Clarence Clark, M.P. by Edgar Wallace

Richard Horatio Edgar Wallace was born on the 1st April 1875 in Greenwich, London. Leaving school at 12 because of truancy, by the age of fifteen he had experience; selling newspapers, as a worker in a rubber factory, as a shoe shop assistant, as a milk delivery boy and as a ship's cook.

By 1894 he was engaged but broke it off to join the Infantry being posted to South Africa. He also changed his name to Edgar Wallace which he took from Lew Wallace, the author of Ben-Hur.

In Cape Town in 1898 he met Rudyard Kipling and was inspired to begin writing. His first collection of ballads, The Mission that Failed! was enough of a success that in 1899 he paid his way out of the armed forces in order to turn to writing full time.

By 1904 he had completed his first thriller, The Four Just Men. Since nobody would publish it he resorted to setting up his own publishing company which he called Tallis Press.

In 1911 his Congolese stories were published in a collection called Sanders of the River, which became a bestseller. He also started his own racing papers, Bibury's and R. E. Walton's Weekly, eventually buying his own racehorses and losing thousands gambling. A life of exceptionally high income was also mirrored with exceptionally large spending and debts.

Wallace now began to take his career as a fiction writer more seriously, signing with Hodder and Stoughton in 1921. He was marketed as the 'King of Thrillers' and they gave him the trademark image of a trilby, a cigarette holder and a yellow Rolls Royce. He was truly prolific, capable not only of producing a 70,000 word novel in three days but of doing three novels in a row in such a manner. It was estimated that by 1928 one in four books being read was written by Wallace, for alongside his famous thrillers he wrote variously in other genres, including science fiction, non-fiction accounts of WWI which amounted to ten volumes and screen plays. Eventually he would reach the remarkable total of 170 novels, 18 stage plays and 957 short stories.

Wallace became chairman of the Press Club which to this day holds an annual Edgar Wallace Award, rewarding 'excellence in writing'.

Diagnosed with diabetes his health deteriorated and he soon entered a coma and died of his condition and double pneumonia on the 7th of February 1932 in North Maple Drive, Beverly Hills. He was buried near his home in England at Chalklands, Bourne End, in Buckinghamshire.

Index of Contents

I

NOBBYNATION

"Me father," said Nobby Clark, thoughtfully, "in a manner of speakin' was one of the practicalest chaps you could imagine. He was one of them keen, grey-eyed men with business ability that you read about nowadays when the Tariff Reform candidate is bein' described by his favourite reporter. He had the country at heart; he used to carry a bit of it about in his pocket to chuck at any stray policeman he happened to see.

"When he saw our trade dwindlin', an' foreign-made goods comin' in to compete with British-made goods, he used to cry like a child.

"'Tariff Reform,' he used to say, 'means work for all—who want it. It means More Hands Wanted. I can see the day a-comin',' he sez, enthusiastic, 'when I shall be wearin' me boots out gettin' out of the way of work. An' what will that mean? More work for the shoemaker, more work for the pavement maker, more work for the manufacturer of police whistles. O England!' he sez, with tears in his eyes, 'oh, me country—as far as I know.'

"That's how elections always took father. I remember the last election. He was very bitter.

"'What!' he sez, tremblin' with emotion, 'what!' he sez, 'can I sleep in me bed at night with the thought of them poor Javanese fellers a-slavin' in the mines of Johannysburg? Is this what I might have died for, if I'd been a soldier—only I had more sense—is this what I squandered me blood an' treasure for?' he sez, horrow-stricken; 'is this the miners' war that me right honourable friend the member for Birmingham spoke of? Mr. Speaker, in the name of Humanity—whose address for the moment escapes me memory—in the name of our sacred Liberty! In the name of Wilberforce, and them other famous cocoa merchants—I protest!'

"I can see him now," said Nobby reflectively, "a little the worse for drink, but patriotic, holdin' on to a lamp-post an' addressin' his constituents.

"'Will you tax the people's food?' he sez, sternly. 'Will you take the bread out of the mouths of babes an' sucklin's? Will you rob the young an' the innercent of their beer? What did me right honourable friend, Mr. Gladstone, say in 1879? He sez, gentlemen of the jury, that your food will cost you more! 'Oh England,' he sez, anguishedly, 'Oh Ireland, Scotland, Wales, an' the Isle of Man! Is it for this brave Cobden fell gloriously fightin'?—if I'm wrong I will ask you to correct me—was it for this—'

"Then a copper would come an' shift him, an' father would return home very hurried.

"Father had these here moments of poetical feelin', if I may use the expression, because he was naturally of a poetical turn of mind. I never knew a feller who could turn out poetry like me Father—that was why he was such a popular feller at elections.

"There wasn't any subject me father couldn't write poetry about. He'd write poetry to the landlord when he was asked for his rent; he'd write kind poetry, an' hard-hearted poetry.

"I shall never forget the poem he wrote to the landlady at the 'Star an' Mitre'' when he was falsely accused of pinchin' pots. It was in all the papers:

"'Oh woman with the serpent's tongue!
Oh blonmin' clever Mrs. Bung!'

"it started. I can only remember little bits of it:

"'Thy lies would put me in the dock;
Thy face would nearly stop a clock;
Thy evidence would get me hung,
Oh woman with the serpent's tongue!'

"It created a rare sensation that poem. The landlady was goin' to summon me father for defamation of character, an' our local paper took it up, an' a young poet named Cornelius Ox (that's as unlikely a name as I can think of) wrote a reply:

"'Oh poet with a funny face,
It's nearly time you knew your place,
Oh poet with the coward's pen,
Retire into your loathsome den.'

"The history of that controversy—if you will forgive the vulgar word,"—said Nobby, solemnly, "will be remembered for many years. Poem follered poem in rapid succession. Me father took up a position on the enemy's flank, an' sent verse after verse from his famous quick-firin' fountain pen, an' the enemy retorted briskly. On the Monday mornin' me father got the range an' dropped a sonnet into the trenches, but Cornelius Ox, rapidly takin' cover, sniped me father with a little trifle entitled 'An Ode to a Piece of Dirt.' Though sorely harassed, me father replied gallantly, an' a limerick which began 'There once was a dud named Ox, Who never changed his sox,' was aimed with deadly precision.

"I forget how the battle ended, but you can be sure of one thing: Me father won.

"But it wasn't only because he was a great poet that me father was, in a manner of speakin', in such demand. He was, to use a foreign expression, an orator. He was the feller to move an audience! If you turned the hose on 'em, you couldn't move 'em quicker than me father did. There was his famous speech at Limehouse—you've heard of that? Never mind about anybody else, it was me father that made Limehouse famous.

"'What!' he sez, 'shall we groan under the tyranny of the turnip-headed lords? (Cries of No, no!) Shall we put back the clock of progress to closin' time?—(cheers)—or shall we march triumphant to glory or thereabouts, over the mangled remains of the enemies of the people?'"

(The speaker resumed his seat amidst loud an' continued cheerin', the right hon. gentleman havin' spoken for an hour an' twenty-three minutes by Greenwich time).

"Somebody ought to make a collection of me father's speeches; he'd look well in a nice red cover, an' gilt edges—the speeches I mean."

"One of the first signs of a general election is the rush they make for him. Both sides have a cut. For a day or two all is suspense. Which side will Clark go on? People walk about the streets scarcely darin' to hope. Little groups stand at the street corners. Will me father sign on for the Millwall Tariff Reform Team, or will he throw in his lot with the Manchester United Lord Lamers? The newspaper bills come out every half hour: 'Has Clark joined the M.U.L.L.?' 'Sinister Rumours about Clark.' At eleven o'clook at night the news is out! 'Clark signs on for the M.T.R.!'

"The feelin' is too tense for cheerin'; strong men shake hands not trustin' theirselves—or each other—to speak. A great sigh goes up. The spell of suspense is broken; the traffic is resumed.

"'It has been an anxious time (writes our special correspondent). First one side, then the other, seemed to gain an advantage, but the strong man standin' with one hand gracefully restin' on the zinc counter of the private bar an' his other leg crossed, stood emotionless. Ever an' anon, he would, in the absent-minded manner of the truly great, attempt to drink out of an empty glass, an' one of those present would immediately order the glass to be refilled, Mr. Clark thankin' him with a gentle smile; this amusin' lapse on the part of the honoured gentleman occurred twenty or thirty tines durin' the evenin'—truly, even the Great Ones of the Earth have human weaknesses!'

"The deed is done, me father is adopted, there's a last despairin' effort by the cursed opposition. Can they get him transferred to their team? Can he be disqualified for foul tactics an' warned off the field? No, the die is cast, he's burnt his boots, he's crossed the what-d'-ye-call-it.

"North an' south, east an' west, the message is flashed. The gold miner on the Gold Coast, sittin' on a nugget, reads the news an' wipes his horny brow; the Arctic explorer sittin' on the North Pole reads the news an' buries his face in his hands. Clark is standin'! Clark has been nominated for Millwall!

"An' now begins what I might call the stern business of the campaign. The first thing me father does is to borrow a bit on account. The next thing is to find out what the election's about. He buys a newspaper. Horrow! 'Jerry M. fell at the last fence but two'—no, that isn't it. He looks in another part of the paper! 'A farthin' damages'—no, that can't be it. Ah! here it is. 'Tariff Reform means hard labour for all.' Me father grasps the deadly significance an' hesitates. Is it worth the sacrifice? Will they make him work! Can they, any way? I think not.

"An' now the newspapers are pourin' forth their scurrilous abuse, or just appreciation.

"What does the Milwall Kicker say?

"Mr. Clark embodies all the virtues of John Bright, Joseph Chamberlain, and Mr. Barnum. He is one of England's brightest hopes—we're the other one. When we gaze upon his classic face—whether high classic or no classic, we leave our readers to judge—we are reminded of Julius Caesar's well-known remark:

"The Elliman's was so rubbed in him
That naturally you say to all the world
Is this a man?"'

"But all the comments ain't quite as favourable. There's the Tottenham Hotspur Tidin's, an' the Chelsea Wonders Globe.

"Says the Tidin's:

"'We congratulate Millwall upon its purchase. Ha, he—excuse us laughin'—ha, ha! Who is the disreputable dog with the funny face who has escaped from Wandsworth Goal an' offers himself as a candidate for Millwall? We will open our readers' eyes.

"Carence Clark was convicted at the Middlesex Sessions...' (here follows a list of convictions); 'turn over the page an' begin at the top of the third column. We have shown enough, we hope, to prove that the impudent...' (two columns of low abuse).

"What does the Globe say? The Globe is Independent:

"'We think,' sez the "Globe," 'that it is quite possible that Millwall has chosen wisely. On the other hand it is quite possible that it hasn't. You never can tell. We have nothin' to say against Mr. Clark. At the same time we've nothin' to say in his favour. Let us leave the question there, desirin', as we do, to maintain a statesman-like attitude.'

"The campaign begins in earnest. Wherever me father goes he is follered by a cheerin' crowd throwin' bokays, some of 'em tastefully got up to look like bricks, an' weighin' as much as seven pounds.

"On all walls an' hoardin's bills appear by magic:

"'VOTE FOR CLARENCE CLARK, THE FRIEND OF THE PEOPLE.'

"an' in little letters underneath:

"'Who Vote For Him.'

"Will Clark win? That is the question on every tongue. Will he pull down the Government majority an' give a line to the country?

'Interviewed by our special political correspondent, Mr. Clark said:

"'We are winnin' all along the line: Everywhere I meet with encouragement in me arduous an' difficult campaign. I am fightin' a fight for England. I am fightin' for clean finance—an' even dirty finance as long as it's money. Will I abolish prisons? You may tell your readers that that is the first plank in me bed: Am I in favour of blokes for women? I am. What's my opinion about the Navy? It's a splendid idea. I wonder nobody thought of it before. Yes," sez Mr. Clark in conclusion, "I am a supporter of the House of Lords. I believe in it havin' a free hand: I don't approve of the tied-house system—you never know whether you're talkin' to the Bung or the Barman.'"

"Pop'lar feelin' runs higher an' higher: the Milwall Kicker publishes me father's oughtto-be-ography.

"'Our fearless candidate is the son (we hope) of the late Sir Swaffer Clark, of Clark Hall, Clerkenwell, E.C. Born at a very early age, the brilliant politician grew with such rapidity that he was 21 before his elder brother had reached 16. His record of public service is a splendid one. Inspector of Pavements 1880-1890. Inspector of Prisons 1890-'91 (six months), '92 (three months), '93 (twelve months)—an' honourably mentioned at the Assizes, an' so forth.'

"In this brief an' hurried way," said Nobby Clark, "I sketch, if I may say so, the beginnin' of me father's campaign, a campaign that shook, so to speak, the political world to its foundations.

"Of how me father held his first big meetin' with me right honourable friend Arthur Balfour in the chair, of how he scotched the old-age pension lie, an' what he said about Lloyd George we will tell next week."

II

THE MASS MEETING

"When we left me father last week," said Nobby Clark, "he was havin' a drink with his agent. So I didn't happen to mention the fact: it's true, all the same. Whenever I don't tell you what me father was doin', you can put him down in the private bar of 'The Bald-Headed Stag.'

"The campaign had commenced. Millwall was stirred to its dep's; it was announced that a mass meetin' would be held addressed by me Right Honourable friend Smith. Have you ever seen Smith? He looks like eighteen an' talks like eighty.* He's the boy for the Socialists.

[* Can this be F. E. Smith?]

"'A gentleman in the audience sez, "Rot!" he sez. (Laughter.) 'Would he mind obligin' us with his address as well as his name?' (Loud laughter, in which the Right Honourable gentleman joined.)

"That's the sort of feller Smith is. Balfour is another feller. What a man! What a memory!

"'Me hon. an' gallant friend with the false teeth,' he sez, 'asks me to define me position. (Cheers.) I wouldn't if I could an' I couldn't if I would;' an' whilst the audience is thinkin' the answer out, the Right Honourable gentleman slid down the rain pipe into the street.

"It's useless for me," explained Nobby, "to go through the list of me father's leaders. You've probably heard of 'em. There's the Right Honourable Austen.

"'In 1762,' he sez, 'we imported twenty-three million pounds worth of motor-cars—(cries of "Shame"); in 1862 that import had fallen to £21,764,861 (sensation); in 1893, we exported £7,741,099 worth of bootlaces (a voice: "Horse-hair!"). A gentleman sez "Horse-hair!" (Cheers.) Let me tell that gentleman that if they were Horse-hair laces they were taken from the hard-worked tails of British horses!' (Deafenin' cheers, the band playin' "Rule Britannia.")

"Me father entered into the fight with what I might call alacrity.

"'What you've got to do,' sez the Conservative agent, 'is keep your eye open for old-age pensions.'

"'How many?' sez me father very eager.

"'What I mean to say is,' sez the agent, 'you've got to watch the other side, or they'll be doin' you a shot in the eye.'

"'I'm there,' sez me father, 'if wanted; if wanted,' he sez, 'I'm there.'

"An' sure enough he was.

"It wasn't long after the election started, me father heard a sort of rumour about old-age pensions.

"'I'll stop that lie,' he sez, an' standin' up at the bar he wrote very rapid. In two twinks there was a handbill on the streets:—

OLD AGE PENSION LIE

It has been stated that I,
Clarence Clark, am in
favour of
old age pensions.

THIS IS A LIE!

"Father was very proud of that handbill, until the election agent came round to see him...Blue in the face, the election agent was.

"'You've ruined the election!' he yells; 'oh, you butter basket! Oh, you tripe-faced, cow-headed turnip.'

"'What's up, me right honourable friend?' sez me father, turnin' pale.

"'What's up?' sez the agent jumpin' about an' tearin' his hair. 'You've said the very thing you oughtn't have said—you're in favour of old-age pensions!'

"'Am I?' sez me father; 'then,' he sez, very stern, 'why didn't you tell me?'

"But me father knew too much about politics to be upset about a little thing like that. In twenty minutes there was another bill out:—

DASTARDLY FORGERY!
ATTEMPT TO DISCREDIT CLARK!

Whereas, a certain bill has been
circulated supposed to have
been written by me, clarence
clark, an' sayin' I am against
old-age pensions,

THIS IS ANOTHER LIE!!

"'How's that?' sez me father.

"'Fine,' sez the agent. 'You're too good for politics; you ought to have been workin' out astronomical calculations for Dr. Cook.'

"But it was a close thing for me father, an' when he went round on Saturday to draw his wages from the Parliament'ry Factory he had a talk to the agent.

"'I shalt have to read it up,' sez me father, shakin' his head, 'these new things puzzle me—why, a feller asked me yesterday whether I was in favour of Tariff Reform.'

"'What did you say?' sez the agent, gettin' palpitation of the heart.

"'I sez,' sez me father, 'that I believed in vaccination—which is the same thing.'

"'Quite right,' sez the agent, an' handed over me father's salary.

"'Here!' sez me father, countin' it, 'what d' ye call this?'

"'There's been certain stoppages,' sez the agent. 'You lost a quarter the other evenin'—not turnin' up to a meetin'. Then yer was fined ten shillin's for not bowin' to a duke when you met him. We've got to be strict like this,' he sez, 'owin' to the other candidates: if we showed you any fav'ritism they'd take liberties.'

"'But,' sez me father, countin' the money again.

"It's all right,' sez the agent, 'you're no worse off than the hon. member for Tarbury—we fined him 40s. for wearin' a made-in-Germany shirt.'

"Anybody who knew me father would have been alarmed by his (if you'll allow me to use the expression) ominous silence.

"He took the money an' went home.

"Everywhere there was signs of his popularity. Bills on every wall, fellers givin' away handbills, people hootin' him in the street, an even the little children playin' with monkeys-on-sticks painted to look like him.

"What me father did that evenin' will never be known. Certain papers have published certain reports, but what happened is still secret.

"It was the night of the meetin'. Me hon. an' gallant friend, Mr. Balfour, was in the chair, wearin' his famous orchard in his coat, an' an eyeglass in each eye. Me right hon. but learned friend, Mr. Walter Solong, was there, but it was not to see them the intelligent men of England went, nor the unintelligent either.

"The flower of English shivalry (I don't know what that means, but no offence is meant), was gathered.

"'It was a night,' wrote me friend, Bart Kennedy, 'a night of wonder; of dukes; of wonderful dukes; a night of knights; a knight-night.'

"The night of the meetin' has come at last. It's been the subject of conversation on all hands for weeks. Old men, an' young men, an' little children—me father's name's on their lips.

"'If you don't go to sleep,' sez the mother of the family, 'Mr. Clark will come an' frighten you.'

"The approaches to the hall are crowded. As carriage after carriage rolls up, cheers an' hoots make night hijeous.

"'On the platform (writes our political correspondent) I saw me Lord Duke of Everton, lookin' very pretty in his scarlet bed-gown trimmed with white rabbit skin, an' havin' the tippets worn very low. Me Lord Duke de Leicester Fosse looked radiant in his new coronet an' carried the family sword, a pretty custom which many of higher-class ducal families are revivin' in these perilous days. Dressed in sequins, with wide reveres of torchon lace an' old gold panels, the Duke of Shuffield-Wednesbury was talkin' with the Marquis de Tottenham-Hotspur—who was lookin' very young in pink stockings. Many of the peers had brought their escuteons with them—the weather bein' very unpromisin', but the young Duke of Millwall wore a flesh-coloured mackintosh with a wealth of nuns' veilin', an' the effect was extremely dainty.

"'It was a brilliant an' a dazzlin' sight, an' many of the common people were reduced to tears.

"'As they came pourin' into the vast hall I could hear, amidst their grateful cries, the stern, earnest fellers sayin' to one another "Don't crush me—or you'll break the eggs," an' another, "Can I have half of your brick, Harry?" an' such like humorous an' good- natured remarks.

"'"We have met here," sez Mr. Balfour, strokin' his beard, "to strike a blow for freedom. (Cheers.) When I say freedom," he sez, "I mean for liberty. (Cheers an' counter-cheers.) Me own position is clear: What I have said I have read." (Loud and prolonged cheerin'.)

"'"What is the position of England to-day? (Cries of 'No, No.') A gentleman sez No! (Laughter.) I answer his question most emphatically in the affirmative." (Loud an' prolonged cheerin' durin' which the right hon. gentleman resumed his seat).

"'Here (writes our political correspondent) was a lead for England! What a clarion cry for our country! Here was the note of battle, a rallyin' cry for the strong forces of our beloved party!

"But what a scene when me father was assisted on to the platform by two friends!

"What deafenin' cries rose to the roof when, staggerin' slightly under the stress of emotion, he started straight away with the speech of the evenin'.

"'Gentlemen,' sez me father, swayin' from side to side, 'I've got a few words to say to you.'

"There was deafenin' applause.

"'What I've got to say,' sez me father, 'is this: A fair day's work for a fair day's pay an' no bloomin' stoppages. (Cheers.) I've got to work for me livin',' sez me father, burstin' into tears an' leanin' very heavy on the chairman, 'Oh, heavens!' he sez, 'nobody lo-oves me-e!'

"'I'm a Socialist by birth,' he sez, an' Mr. Balfour jumped.

"'Fetch a policeman!' he gasps.

"'I'm as good an any duke,' sez me father, fiercely, 'or duchess,' he sez, 'an' I ask you one an' all to join with me in singin'

"The land! the land! the groun' on which we stand."

"'Are you mad?' hisses the election agent.

"'No,' sez me father, 'but I've got me transfer—I'm playin' for them friends of liberty an' labour, the Lib'rals (cries of "Cad!" from the dukes)—who don't,' he sez, 'deduct quarters from me hard-earned screw. Frien's,' he sez, addressin' the audience, 'I invite you to hear me tomorrow evenin' deliver me famous address on "Dukes I have Bit"—me honourable friend, Kier Hardie, in the chair.'

"This," said Nobby, "was the second stage of me father's political career. I don't know how he got out of the hall alive. One duke hit him with a sword, an' another made a face at him, but two policemen got father out somehow, an' took him home in a p'lice amb'lance."

Next week Mr. Clark takes the field as a Radical with Nihilistic tendencies, supported by the Right Hon. Lloyd, the Right Hon. Winston. and many other notable personages.—Editor.

III

A RADICAL CHANGE

"Me father had one good point," said Nobby Clark. "He always stuck to his convictions as long as he had 'em. The moment he hadn't got any, he got a new lot in: he wasn't one of them fellers that got his convictions by the half hundred-weight, an' had to open his cupboard every time he heard the coal man shoutin', 'Who'll buy my nobbly?'—'he got 'em by the ton an' paid at the end of the month.

"When me father took up a position on a subject, you couldn't make him budge, especially if he had a drop of drink in him an' when he decided to chuck the Millwall Tariff Reform Team, an' sign on for the Manchester United Lord-lamers, he knew what he was doin'.

"But the excitement was tremendous! Bulletins was issued every half-hour. At eight o'clock the next mornin' me father took up his new position.

"'Good-bye,' he sez, with tears in his eyes, to the young lady behind the bar of his committee room, 'it breaks me heart to part from these here gilded halls of vice,' he sez—he always used to use the private bar of the Risin' Sun. 'Good-bye,' he sez, 'the people call me, England wants me.'

"'Where are you goin', Mr. Clark?' sez the young lady behind the bar.

"'To the bottle an jug department,' sez me father, heroic.

"That day the Lord-lamers' agent come to me father.

"'Well, Mr. Clark,' he sez, rubbin' his hands, 'we've got to get busy. What about your manifesto?'

"'The last time I see him run,' sez me father, reflectfully,' was at Armatree seven years ago: a good old horse he was. He ought to have won the National—'

"'I'm talking' politics,' sez the agent nastily; 'what about your address to the electors?'

"'Same old address,' sez me father, '92, Poverty Court; 'phone I.O.U. Central.'

"After the agent had said a few bitter things about comic candidates, me father got down to business. A representative of the Tottenham Kicker had a few minutes' conversation with the honourable gentleman.

"Sez that journal:

"'If last week we described the gallant candidate as a bottle-nosed mud-shoveller, we did it under a misapprehension as to the views of the noble-minded patriot which is now standin' in the Socialist interest.'

"'Yes,' sez the hon. gent., 'it is a tryin' campaign. I'm fightin' for the people. 'Oh, the people!' sez the hon. gent. with tears in me eyes. 'Oh, the hard-workin' sons of toil! When I think,' he sez, 'of the amount of work that's done in this country by people who ought to know better me brain reels. Do I believe in taxin' the rich? I do: I'm poor. Do I believe in abolishin' the Lords? I do: I'm not a lord. Do I believe in death duties? I do: I'm still alive.'

"That same evenin' me father addresses a meetin' at Limehouse-street.

"Me father rises amidst scenes of tremendous excitement; sobs are heard on every hand, even the reporters are quiverin' with emotion an' cold feet. What will he say? What message goes forth to the country?

"Me father's lips are seen to be movin'. 'Instantly,' sez our descriptive reporter in his original way, 'a dense silence fell upon the proleteriat.'

"Me father raises his hand.

"'Llandidrod harlech flewellen, look you,' he sez; 'an' the audience rises an' screams enthusiastic. Some fall to the floor gnashin' their teeth with joy, some burst with tears an' are led out; some faint, some feel sick.

"At last the cheerin' subsides.

"'I must apologise,' see me father, 'for usin' me own language. (Cheers.) Me heart is in me native Wales. (Loud an' prolonged cheerin'.) Oh, Wales!' he sez, 'thy hills, thy mountains, thy mines of best steamin' coals: Wales!' he sez, workin' himself into a frenzy, 'home of the welcher from times immoral, land of poetry an' song,' he sez, 'an' dance. Birthplace of Jimmy Welch an' other poets—(cheers)—I greet thee!'

"The speaker went on to refer to the Budget.

"'They don't like me in the House of Lords,' he sez, 'an' I will tell you why.' (A voice: "Don't trouble.")

"'Gentlemen,' he sez, 'I'll give you a few facts: At Holloway, in London, there's a baronial mansion. (Cheers.) It covers four acres of land an' a bit. (Cries of "Shame!")

"'Well, now, that baronial castle is owned by the Crown, an' the people who live in it pay no rates. (Sensation.)

"'Well, now, right opposite that castle is a little draper's shop called Selfridge's. (More sensation.) Well, now, that shop pays hundreds a year in rates. ("Disgraceful!")

"'Well, now, when I tell you that this little draper's shop only covers four square yards of ground you'll understand me intense disgust for facts. They don't like me Facts in the Lords. (Laughter.) They prefer the truth. ("No, no!")

"'Well, now, I said that this little drapers shop was opposite to Holloway Castle; when I say "opposite," I mean you can get there in an hour by motor bus. When I think of this little draper's shop coverin' four square yards—or four thousand; I'm not quite certain to a yard or two, an' any way it doesn't effect the case—when I think of this little draper's shop payin' hundreds of pounds, me heart bleeds. (Cheers.)

"'Well, now, I will give you another case. The Lords don't like me facts. (Laughter.) They don't like 'em because they can't prove 'em.' (Cheers.)

"Then me father goes on talk of the shockin' way the Lords who own Wormwood Scrubbs put upon their tenants.

"'Me heart aches,' sez me father, 'for these unfortunate people. The Lords must go! (Loud an' continued cheers.) You can't make om'lettes without poachin' eggs. (Cheer.) I'm a poacher meself. Often,' he sez, 'in me natural Wales, when I've seen the little Welsh rabbits skippin' about on the banks an' braes of Llangenathrens-hargachinel, jumpin' from letter to letter, I've gallantly follered the ferocious animals an' tackled 'em in their lair. (Cheers.) But as I was sayin', the Lords must go. I don't know where, but they've got to go. (Cheers.)

"'Well, now, we come to the question of death duties, in other words the tax on cigarettes. Who smokes cigarettes?—the dukes. (Loud cheers.) An' whilst these gilded popinjays are smokin' cigarettes, what are their sweated tenants smokin'> Gentlemen,' sez me father solemnly, 'they are smokin' bacon.' (Cries of horror.)

"'Well, now,' sez me father, 'I see in front of me a number of Free Church ministers. (Sympathetic cheers,) I recognise 'em by their side whiskers. Well, now, I say to you that me policy is a good Sunday-go-to-meetin' policy. It's easier for a camel to get the needle than it is for a rich man to get the hump. What I like about the Free Church,' sez me father, 'is its impartiality; it's all on my side; it's impartial to the other side. That's fair. Gentlemen,' sez me father, in conclusion, 'you're at the partin' of the ways—I don't know what it means, but there you are, you're there. Will you tax food? he sez: 'will you put a tax upon bread?' he sez. 'We promised you the big loaf—you've of it. We couldn't increase the size, so we've put up the price.'

"'Gentlemen,' sez me father, 'let us vote accordin' to our feelin's. Judge the case fairly, an' vote for me.' (The right hon. gentleman resumed his seat amidst scenes of uproarious applause.)

"Me father is now overwhelmed with work. How does he spend his day? Read the article in M.A.C. (Mainly about Clark).

"'I remember (writes me noble friend, T.P., the member for Liverpool), when I first met Clarence Clark he was a bright young member. Eager, alert, he was the life an' soul of the refreshment room. In those dark days of 1886 when the destinies of Ireland trembled in the balance...He rises at four o'clock in the mornin', an' without wastin' his time by washin' he immediately summonses his two secretaries. The correspondence of the day is rapidly gone through, all the postal orders bein' put on one side an' the letters burnt. At seven be takes a cup of coffee at a neighbourin' coffee stall. He follows this up by makin' a series of visits to neighbouring houses. At nine he has breakfast at the Blue Lion—sometimes two glasses, sometimes three; at ten he has a consultation with his agent, which may take any time up to three hours It all depends whether the agent parts readily...'

"What me father does in these days few people realise. They don't know the work, or the anxiety of the strain.

"Me father addresses a meetin' of Old Age Pensioners at Bungley Hall.

"It is a movin' scene. The audience is carried into the hall on shutters. Me father marches into the hall behind two bagpipers, an' on risin' is greeted with cheers an' counter cheers.

"'When the great lawyer rose' sez the frozen-out racin' reporter of the "Tottenham Kicker," '6 to 4 was freely offered an' taken that he'd be killed. He made a slow start, but, warmin' to his work, he joined the leaders turnin' into the straight an', comin' through his horses, he drew to the front, bein' never afterwards headed.'

"'Ma frien's,' sez me father. 'A'm verra glad tae see ye here the nicht, d'ye ken. Ma wee frien', Winston Chur-r-chill—(ironical laughter)—wisna able to come, sae A've droppit in tae mak' a few remarks about auld age peensions. (Cries of "Bravo, Harry Lauder!") An' now,' sez me father, resumin' his speech in pure English, 'I come to an important question. (Cheers.) It's the question of Old Age Pensions. (Hear, hear.) If the Tories return you'll not get 'em. (Sensation.) Me right honourable friend, Balfour— (groans)—was only tellin' me the other day. "Clarence," he sez, "if we come back we'll take away them pensions." "What," sez I, "will you give 'ern instead?" "Six months," sez me right hon. friend. (Hisses.)

"'That's how the position stands,' sez me father, 'only worse. When I think,' he sez, 'of the pore old fellers with money in the bank, who will be deprived of the opportunity of livin' on the taxpayer me heart is stirred with profound anguish.'

"'An',' he sez, 'I'll tell you somethin' more. If the Tories return your front gardens will be converted into deer forests for the effete nobility. (Sensation.) I know this is a fact, because a man I met in the train told me so.' (Cheers.)

"'Let us take the question of Dreadnoughts. (Hisses.) What's the good of 'em? (Bravo.) Can a Dreadnought plough the land? ("Bravo.") Can a Dreadnought wipe the eye of a sorrerful orphan? ("No, no.") Can a Dreadnought pay the tally man? (Emotion.) Then, down with Dreadnoughts, an' up with pensions.' (Loud an' continued cheerin'.)

"The speech caused a wave of feelin' throughout the country.

"Mr. Balfour, speakin' at the Society for Providin' Hats for Terriers, said:

"'Speakin' of rats (laughter)—I have read a speech by the Lord Advocate for Millwall. I have nothin' to say against the right hon. gentleman except that he's a liar. (Cheers.) He's dishonoured his country, if any, he's dishonoured his profession (unknown). He's dishonoured his party—whatever it may be. He's a frigid an' calculated, hard-boiled shop-egg liar. (Cheers.) Let us, if we can, preserve the decencies of debate. (Cheers.) Let us keep the tone of this election as high as possible. Do not let us be lured into abuse by a pot-headed thief whose only claim to distinction is that he has escaped the gallows.' (Loud an' prolonged cheerin', durin' which the right hon. gentleman resumed his seat.)

"Speakin' at Birmingham, on the followin' day, the Right Hon. Austen referred to me father's statement.

"'Never,' he sez, 'in me long an' varied political career have I read much a speech. (Cheers.) I can prove the Right Hon. Clarence Clark to be a liar. In 1874 we imported £10,000,000 worth of brass buttons; our exports of dog biscuits for that same year was £8,725,000—a difference of a million an' a quarter. (Sensation.) What does that prove? It proves that brass button are goin', dog biscuits are goin', an' I say to you, gentlemen, that our duty is to make the foreigner Pay! (Uproarious applause.)

"'Let us consider the question of Old Age Pensions. In 1821 we imported 2,000 bath chairs, in 1909 we imported £2,000,000 of bath chairs, our exports for a correspondin' period included £1,000,000 worth of Everton toffee, £2,000,000 worth of bassinettes. That shows we are gettin' old. (Cheers.) I say to you that England is losin' her grip on the markets of the world; Tariff Reform means too young at ninety.'

"Me father makes no reply. He is preparin' for the comin' contest. The day of the tight is at hand."

IV

"We left me father," said Nobby, "at the height of his fame; we left him with his words ringin' throughout the land; the election is as good as over; me father is as good as an M.P., or any other man. The leaders crowd round him an' shakes his hand.

"'Clarence,' sez the Right Hon. Askwith, 'You've routed 'em—you've smashed 'em—there's a place in the Cabinet waitin' for you; will you have it boiled or fried? Would you like a pension or a title, or a box of cigars, say the word.'

"'Clarence,' see the Right Hon. Askwith, speakin' under stress of great emotion, 'You've saved the party, me bein' the party; you've lifted England from the hog-tub of despair an' put her in the dust-bin of oratory. Will you be Home Secretary or Not at Home Secretary? Will you be speaker or Spoken-to? Do you desire the wealth of India poured into your lap, or would you rather have a free pass to the White City?'

"An ordinary man would have lost his head, surrounded as he was by the leadin' lights of social reform, but me father only lost his watch.

"'No,' he sez, wavin' 'em aside with a lofty kind of air. 'No,' he sez, 'I desire no reward-(cheers)—not to speak of,' he sez. 'I am only doin' me duty,' he sez, 'an' all cheques an' postal orders should be crossed London an' South-Eastern Bank, an' addressed to me personally.'

"As pollin' day grows nearer an' nearer me father grows in popularity. The cursed Tories an' Food Taxers do their best to show him up. They publish a list of his convictions, they make his landlord summons him for his rent—he only owed for three years—they get the water company to cut off his water, they send a man every day to collect the money from the gas meter in case he pinches it for election expenses; in fact, they persecute me father somethin' shockin'. They even insult him by offerin' him a regular job.

"But me father continued speakin'.

"He addressed a meetin' in Welsh at the Prince of Wales's Tavern. He addressed a meetin' in Irish at the Dublin Arms, an' he addressed several in Scotch at various public places.

"'I've found out,' sez me father, 'the secret of gettin' on in politics. What you've got to do is to talk about gallant little Wales, an' bonny Scotland, an' down-trodden Ireland—the other country don't count.'*

[* Mr. Clark would seem to have hit upon a great political fact.—E.W.]

"'Nobody is interested about England,' sez me father. 'England!' he sez, bitterly, 'the hated Sasser-Knack! The robber an' murtherer of Irish liberty! What about Daniel O'Conner? (I think that was the feller's name.) What about Daniel Lambert, whose blood,' he sez, 'stained his college green? What about the Battle of the Boil? What about me gallant frien' Captain Boycott who was shot by the Thraitors of Donnybrook? Oh, Ireland,' sez me father, 'land of greens an' potatoes, an' pigs. Oh, Erin, Me Vaureen!' (The right hon. gentleman broke down an' could not proceed for some minutes).

"'An' what of Wales?' he sez, 'the ancient Britons? Oppressed,' he sez, fiercely, 'by the accursed Saxon. Wales! Homes of the famous singin' competitions, to wit, Easter-fords, home of the LL., birthplace of Mr. Evans—the famous revivalists; land of the milkman, look you!' (The right hon. gentleman burst into tears, an' said he would never desert Wales—never, never, NEVER!)

"'An' now,' sez me father, 'I come to Scotland. Scotland,' he sez, 'home of the marmalade industry an' Bobby Burns. Birthplace of me right hon. friends, Haldane, John Burns, Mr. Ure, Lawborn, an' Mr. Rufus Isaacs. For centuries ground under the heel of the hateful Southerner. For centuries, gentlemen,' sez me father, 'this cursed England has been lurin' our young men from the simple life of Glasgow to the squalid luxury of Park-lane. For centuries it has been takin' our slim wee, laddies of Edinboro' an' transformin' them into fat millionaires of London. Is this right? ("No, no!") Then vote for Clarence Clark, the friend of every country but his own. Remember,' he sez, warnin'ly, 'Every vote against me is a vote for England.'

"But it ain't the speeches that's the difficulty; it's the questions. But there never was a feller as smart with his answers as me father.

"'Can the right hon., or right off gentleman, as the case may be,' sez a voice in the audience, 'tell me who pays the tax on cocoa—the consoomer, the perdoocer, or the other feller?'

"'In answer to that,' sez me father, 'I have to tell you that the tax is paid by the gentleman who lives at No.9.'

"'Who's that?' sez the voice.

"'Inkey,' sez me father. (Laughter.)

"'I'd like to ask the noble lord,' sez another voice, 'whether he's in favour of a tax on soft goods?'

"'No,' sez me father, 'I don't bear you any ill-will!' (Laughter.)

"'If you're returned to Parliament, will you support a Bill for the abolition of public-houses?' sez another.

"'Ask me,' sez me father.

"'I am askin' you,' sez the voice.

"'Keep on askin' me,' sez me father.' (Loud an' uproarious laughter.)

"Sometimes the Tory send a few friends to upset his meetin'.

"The candidate on risin',' sez our very own, body an' soul, correspondent, 'was greeted with booin' an' cat calls. Mr. Clarence Clark said he hoped he was addressin' Englishmen (cries of "Go home!") He appealed to them as Englishmen to listen to him whilst he said a few words about their disgraceful treatment of Ireland. (Uproar.) He observed that there was a large number of the criminal classes present. (Disgraceful disturbance.) He was glad to see so many of 'em at liberty—(Interruption)—but he supposed there had been a fire at Wormwood Scrubbs, an' a good many of them had got away whilst nobody was lookin'. (The rest of the candidate's remarks were inaudible.)'

"But the pollin' day was at hand; nearer an' nearer grew the fatal hour; all business was disorganised; the telegraph wires groaned under the telegrams of encouragement. Me father got so many that he was able to paper the front room with 'em.

"'A HAPPY RETURN.—ASKWITH.'

"'VICTORY LIES YOUR WAY.—URE.'

"'MENTIONED YOU IN MY WORKHOUSE SPEECH.—BURNS.'

"An' similar pleasant greetin's.

"As the day of the poll dawned even the reporters lost their heads. The Hotspur Kicker was so upset that it confused me father with another public character.

"'On the mornin' of the 15th; sez the "Kicker," 'Clarence Clark rose at an early hour an' partook of a hearty breakfast of bread an' cocoa. He thanked the governor an' the warders for the kindness they had showed him, an' expressed his penitence for the crime. He walked with a firm step...'

"There was an awful row about that bit gettin' into the paper, an' six of me father's political supporters, went out lookin' for the chap who wrote it, an' if they'd have found him he wouldn't have walked with a firm step, or any other kind.

"Me father drives from one pollin' booth to another. Everywhere he is greeted with enthusiasm. One man pushes through the crowd to shake him by the hand, changes his mind, an' pinches his watch. Across the streets are banners, 'Hail, Clark. Good luck to thee!' an' such touchin' sentiments as 'The Tarboilers' Association saith Good Luck.'

"The day proceeds. Me father addressee an open-air meetin' at the gasworks.

"'Feller workers,' he sez,' feller citizens of this Empire on which the sun never, or seldom ever, sets, I stand before you to-day, the old reliable firm, carryin' on business as usual. If you return me to Parliament what will it mean? Better prices, no odds-on chances, pay out 1, 2, 3, first past the post. I am in favour of horses for courses, the apprentice allowance for Frank Wootton, an' the abolition of the startin' gate. I am in favour of givin' bookmakers penal servitude, an' of hangin' tic-tak men. We are tremblin', feller workmen,' he sez, speakin' with emotion, 'on the edge of a precipice. In a few days the weights for the Spring Handicaps will be published. Under a Tory Government we shall see Christmas Daisy handicapped with 8st. 7lbs. (Sensation.) We shall see Symon's Pride cruelly handicapped with 8st.' (Groans.) When I look around me, my fellow workers, an' see how blank your lives are, owin' to the stoppin' of the flat racin', me heart bleeds for you, When I see you writin' on little scraps of paper 'Holy War, 1s. to win,' an' I know that Holy War fell two fences from home, I say 'Down with the fences, down with the sticks; flat racin' for flat people all the year round!' (Frantic cheerin').

"The speech causes a tremendous sensation; it is telegraphed all over the country. The Jockey Club has a special meetin' attended by all the leadin' jockeys; me father is warned off an' warned on again. The Kennel Club revokes his licence, the 'Sportsman' publishes his Bruce-Lowe figure, an' proves he belongs to a runnin' family. But all this time me father is workin'. He's puttin' in the final touches. He addresses a crowded meetin' of the Vegetarians' Protection League at their Bean Café.

"'Feller grass-eaters,' he sez, 'as one who was brought up on the milk of the cocoanut, an' lived on turnip tops for years, let me tell you that we stand to-day on the verge of disaster. (Cheers.) If a Tory Government is returned to power, what will happen? Feller Bean-Munchers, they will put a duty on vegetables. (Sensation.) They will take the very parsnips out of our mouths an' wrench the carrot from the lips of the orphan. (Shame!) What did me right honourable friend Balfour (curse him) say the other day? He sez, "I've a steak in the country." I say,' sez me father, passionately, 'I say that Mr. Balfour, it is not meat—I mean meet—that he should flaunt his degradin' beef-eatin' practices in the face of the eaters of honest greens!' (Loud sounds of approval.)

"But the day is nearly over; the last pollers are pollin'. The police are keepin' back the crowd. Me father wanders in an' out of the countin' room, pale but determined. He carries with him, every time he goes in, a little bundle of papers. They are printed for him by a friend, an they're as much like the pollin' paper as makes no difference. You couldn't tell 'em apart. An' each one's marked:—

CLARENCE CLARK.......... X

"Every time he goes in he leaves one of them little bundles absent-mindedly near one of the chaps that's countin'—an' he's in an' out all the night.

"The countin' goes on. Nine o'clock strikes—ten—eleven, an' at last the returnin' officer finishes his arduous (if you'll pardon the expression) labours.

"Me father makes his way to the balcony in front of the Town Hall, so does the other candidate (whom I've forgot to mention).

"The crowd stretches across the road, the excitement is terrific. It passes the time of waitin' by singin' such stirrin' election songs as 'Let's all go down the Strand,' and 'If I-addy I-ay, I-ay.'

"The returnin' officer steps forward amidst indescribable scenes that the 'Hotspur Kicker' took four columns to describe.

"'Feller electors,' sez the returnin' officer, when he got silence, 'the result is:—'

CLARK: 10,976
THE OTHER FELLER: 4,173

(Cheers and counter cheers.)

"'As,' sez the returnin officer, when he got a hearin' again, 'as there's only six thousand voters on the votin' list, an' as 15,000 have voted, I'm inclined to think that some miscreant has been tamperin' with the sacred ballot-box."

"'Shame!' sez me father, very loud.

"'An so,' sez the returnin' officer, 'I declare the election void. An' whilst the town clerk has gone to fetch a policeman to arrest the feller that did it'—he looks hard at me father—'I'll endeavour to interest you by tellin' you the past history of the right honourable gentleman who's now makin' his escape by a back door.'

"I think," said Nobby reflectively, "he must have been referrin' to me father, because he was the only chap who was makin' his escape at that particular moment."

V

CLARK'S POLL PRODUCER

Last week we left Mr. Clark senr. in a perilous position. His candidature had been successful—too successful, for he had polled considerably more votes than there were constituents! The announcement by the returning officer synchronized with the hurried retirement of Mr. Clark.—Editor. Ideas.

"ME father," said Nobby Clark, "had one, what I might call without offence, characteristic. He was always doin' good for people. When I say always, I mean, of'en an' of'en. It came on him at times quite unexpected, like toothache, an' whilst the fits was on, me father was one of the greatest ministerin' angels the world's ever seen. He went all over the shop doin' good. People did their best to stop him.

"When the news went round the neighbourhood that me father had one of his attacks, the neighbourhood used to lock their doors an' let down pieces of string an' a hook from their bedroom winders to take in the milk.

"There wasn't anythin' too hard for father.

"'Its me mission, Ethel,' he used to say to mother. 'I feel it's me duty to help me feller-man.'

"'What's this?' he sez one day, when he saw Mrs. Snooks, who used to live opposite, with a black eye. 'Oh, heavens!' he sez, 'is there a man so base as to strike his wife. Me blood boils at the thought,' an' with that he dashes into the Snooks's house, drags out Mr. Snooks by the hair, an' beats his head on the pavement.

"Wretch!' sez me father,' to strike a woman with anythin' harder than a blackin' brush. Let this be a lesson to you,' he sez. 'No female livin' shall say that Clarence Clark stood by an' saw a lady struck.'

"When pore Mr. Snooks recovered his conscience in the hospital, an' Mrs. Snooks came to from her fit of hysterics, it came out that she got her black eye through fallin' on a piece of orange peel, an' that Snooks never laid his hand on her in his life.

"Knowin' me father's generous impulses, nobody was surprised when he returned from the scene of his arjuous labours. The poll was no sooner declared, with me father as member for the Withy Grove Division of the Manchester United Lord Lamers, than he disappeared. It was the sensation of the day. All the papers came out with special editions:

MISSIN' MEMBER.

MYSTERIOUS DISAPPEARANCE OF A
NOTORIOUS GENTLEMAN.

POLICE CLUES.

"were some of the headin's. People who knew me father was well aware that he'd only disappeared to do somebody a bit of good, an' so he had.

"The feller he was doin' good to was a feller named Clarence Clark.

"'The weary search goes on,' writes the special correspondent of the Witty Wanderer.

"'What has become of our intrepid an' fearless member? No stone has been left unturned to discover his whereabouts; every private bar has been searched, but without result. We are sure that the Hon. Clarence has a complete answer to any slanderous charge in re pollin' papers.'

"After a while me father was found, an' persuaded to return. The four policemen who persuaded him have been on the sick list ever since.

"What will happen?"

"Excitement is intense; public feelin' runs high; it is the topic of conversation. Will he be called before the Stewards an' warned off?

"Will he be disqualified an' the membership handed over to the second? Will he be cautioned as to his future conduct an' his £5 deposit be pinched? Who knows?"*

[* Mr. Clark, sen., seems in some mysterious way to confuse politics with racing.—ED.]

"An objection has been lodged against me father, an' the Stewards are meetin' to consider the matter. All work ceases in the town. Me father's supporters are gatherin' in full strength; the jewellers close their shops an' the police reserves are called out.

"The meetin' meets. The Hotspur Kicker arranges a system of signals to announce the result. Rockets will be fired.

"A red, blue, an' a white rocket means 'Clark disqualified'

"A scarlet, white, an' blue rocket means 'Clark warned off.'

"A crimson, blue, an' white rocket means 'Clark handed over to the police.'

"The Kicker didn't make arrangements for any other signals because they didn't think they was necessary.

"At eleven o'clock the crowd before the Objection Room numbered 50,000, or 50, accordin' to the paper you read about it in. Suddenly a green rocket is fired. (Cheers.)

"It is follered by a yeller rocket. (Counter cheers.) What does it mean? Nobody knows. There is great enthusiasm, an' people who haven't spoken to one another for years are silent.

"Soon the result is out:

"The Stewards called Mr. Clarence Clark before them to explain the election. He wouldn't come, but sent a letter sayin' he was ill. Asked to explain why more people voted for him than lived in the district, the hon. gentleman said they was moral supporters. The Stewards considered the explanation satisfactory an' over-ruled the objection.'

"Me father is in!

"They bring the news to him, at his house, Clark Hall, Clark-street.

"He won't open the door to 'em; he thinks they're the police. They holler the joyful news to him through the keyhole.

"'I dessay,' he hollers back, sarcastic; 'I've heard that yarn before. You ain't goin' to catch me like that.'

"It takes two hours to make him believe it, an' then he goes forth to meet the excited populace. It's a stirrin' scene.

"From every part of the country telegrams an' judgment summonses come pourin' in.

"The lead given by me father is took up all over the shop; telegrams from other candidates come every few minutes.

"'Tell me where you buy your pollin' papers—should like a few,' wires the right hon. member (he hopes) for North Deptford.

"'Since usin' Clark's Patent Poll Extender the population of me district has doubled,' writes the right hon. member (let us trust) for West Albion.

"Me father ain't only famous; he's notorious; his fortune's made; orders come by every post; me father opens a pollin'-paper factory, an' advertises very extensive. Here's one of the advertisements:

Many A Candidate
Has Died
Of worry caused by canvassin',
takin' drinks with other fellers.
Many A Candidate
Has Died
Of fright whilst waitin' for the
result of the election.
Try Clark's Patent Poll
Producers.
Never known to fail; they work
whilst you sleep.

Certificate.
Dear Sir,—
We have analysed the Poll
Producer, an' we find nothin'
injurious to the system, or
likely to bring a blush to the
youngest cheek.
Havum an' Holdum,
C.P., L.P.D.C.; L. an' Y.

"All over the country the result of me father's wonderful discovery is bearin' fruit; sometimes the fruit's a bit overripe; sometimes it's eggs. He's saved the party.

"In the Hobnail Division of Bootshire there was a seat lost to the party. There was 6,000 electors, an' 5,999 voted for the other feller. Did the other feller get in? Thanks to Clark's Poll Producer, he didn't. Me father's factory worked all night on this job, an' the poll was raised from six thousand to sixty thousand, an' the party had a walkover.

"Many excitin' scenes was witnessed. Take the case of Nuttin'ham.

"'As the countin' proceeded,' writes our special photographer an searchlight expert, 'it became oblivious that the Food-taxer would get in, or thereabouts. The Patriotic face of our candidate went red, white an' blue in turn, an' quite a gloom was cast over the community. Suddenly, from outside the Town Hall, came a wild burst of cheerin' an' loud cries of Hurrah!—Clark's Poll Producer had arrived in the knick of time, an' the old Sol of Hope displaced the Jupiter Pluvious of Despair on every countenance.'

"The results began to come in from all sides—father's party was returnin' to power with a big majority. It brought about a change in the candidates: they wasn't as civil as they used to be. They didn't trouble to answer questions.

"'I'd like to ask,' sez a voice at a meetin' in the Tintack Division of Mulford, 'I'd like to ask the more or less honourable gentleman what he thinks of the house of Lords?'

"'Go to blazes,' sez the candidate. 'I can't answer mutton-headed questions like that.'

"'But I'm one of your supporters!' sez a voice.

"'I don't care,' sez the candidate, slappin' his pocket; 'thanks to Clark's Poll Producer I'm independent of dirty-faced fellers like you.'

"He got in with a majority of two millions—father's factory worked overtime for a week.

"In the Brickfield Division of Bath-an'-Wells, another Voice asked the candidate what he thought about Germany.

"'I'm in the proud position,' sez the candidate, 'thanks to a double supply of Clark's Poll Producer, of sayin' we ought to smack Germany.'

"'What!' sez the Voice, very agitated, 'I thought you was against Dreadnoughts?'

"'So I was,' sez the candidate, 'but that was only because I had to kid you to vote for me: thanks to Clark's Poll Pr—'

"Then a brick hit him. Even me father's wonderful invention couldn't stop that.

"The party was in: Right triumphed over Might (or the other way about accordin' to your politics), an' the question rose: What would the party do for father?

"The question, in a manner of speakin', was soon settled. A telegram arrived at Clark Hall in Mr. Askwith's handwritin':

"'Dear Clark,'

sez the telegram,

'Would you like a job as Cabinet Minister? hours, 10 to 4. house, firin', an' uniform provided: duties light; must be a teetotaller an' willin'; no children or followers; fine chance for energetic man; no character required.'

"Me father wired back:

"'TAKE DOWN THE BOARD; I ENGAGE MESELF.'"

VI

CLARK, M.P., CABINET MINISTER

"I think I told you," said Nobby, "that me friends, the Socialists, are back in office; the elections are over; the excitement is dyin' down. The members that are in are payin' their election expenses; the candidates that didn't get in have gone abroad leavin' no address.

"All the Cabinet Ministers are back in town takin' a course of treatment for the throat. The young fellows who've been earnin' fab'lous sums by predictin' the results of the election are now earning fab'lous sums by explainin' why their predictions didn't come off. All the pend'lum swingers, the risin' tiders, an' cetra, are drawin' diagrams to show how their party would have been returned if it hadn't been for the snow storm.

"The elections are over, the country's saved or otherwise, the party of purity an' cats'-meat have detested the cruel food taxers.

"'When I think,' sez me father, addressin' a farewell meetin', 'of the fight we've fought, an' the struggle we've strugged, I shall be glad of the rest that's comin' my way. I'm goin' into a Government office,' he sez very sub-tile. 'All the Cabinet met me father at the station, an' the platform was covered with red lino.

"'Now;' sez Winston, when the cheerin' died away, 'I'd arranged for you to come an' stay with me, but,' he sez, lookin' very hard at me father, owin' to the fact that we've got the carpet up, I can't ask you home just now—I'll arrange with the Speaker for you to have a shakedown in the House—you can sleep on the front Opposition bench, an' fix your shavin' glass on the clerk's table. You can get your meals at Lyons'.'

"'What about when the House sits all night?' sez me father.

"'When I see you yawnin,' sez 'Winston, 'I'll move the adjournment.'

"So that was fixed up.

"'You'd better come round to the lodge,' sez Winston.

"'What lodge,' sez me father.

"'I mean the Cabinet,' sez Winston, we'll have to initiate you proper. It's a solemn business,' he sez, 'makin' a Cabinet Minister. First of all you've got to join our Trade Union.'

"'What's that?" asks me father.

"'The amalgamated an' Associated Society of Front Benchers,' sez Winston, very enthusiastic. 'John Burns started it; it's a great idea. If you get ill an' can't go an' draw your salary, we do it for you, an' allow you sick pay. Every member pays eighteen pence a week an' there is a share out at Easter. Then, every August Bank Holiday,' he sez, more an' more enthusiastic, 'we have an outin'; sometimes by brake an' sometimes by train to the country. It's one of the grandest sights of the year to see us goin' down the Lewisham-road, with me blowin' me own cornet, an' playin' pop'lar tunes.'

"Accordin' to Winston, the idea was to keep out blacklegs, an' keep up the trade union rate of wages for Cabinet Ministers.

"'If we didn't do that,' sez Winston, 'we'd have patriotic fellers who'd take on the job for nothin'.' An' with that he led the way to the lodge room.

"The Cabinet lodge room was one of the strangest places me father had ever seen. It was a big room with all the winder blinds pulled down, an' green lights in the ceilin'. On the right of the Lord High Prime's chair was a big loaf made of gold, an' on the left, a little loaf made of mud, an' above him was a black velvet banner, covered with strange signs, such as pigtails, an' cats'-meat skewers an' rolls of black bread on silver plates. On the left side of the room was a desk covered with red velvet, sparklin' with di'monds, an' little bits of coronets, wot had evidently been recently broken up. There was a red banner over this with a mysterious sign of a church on a hill, an' the words 'How I escaped from the Pretorians—Read it.'

"On the right of the room was another sort of throne, in blue, with a blue banner, containin' the foreign motto:—'En pension,' an' the words 'Great is the truth an' it shall end Ure.'

"'That seat on the left,' sez Winston, careless, 'is mine. I'm the left-handed man of the Cabinet. I've passed through most of the offices, an' hope soon to pass the chair. To tell you the truth,' he says, very confidently, the High Prime ain't the earth.'

"'Ain't he?' sez me father.

"'No;' sez Winston, shakin' his head, 'you'll see a few larks, after you've been here a few lodge nights.'

"Me father went all over the lodge room, admirin' it; by-an'-bye he sez, 'Winston, ole feller, where does me right hon. friend Lloyd sit?'

"Winston winked.

"'He sits on the High Prime,' he sez.

"The night of father's election to the Cabinet came round, an' Winston called for him.

"'I hope you're not nervous?' sez Winston.

"'If I hadn't got plenty of nerve,' sez me father, 'I shouldn't have stood for Parliament.'

"'Quite right,'sez Winston.

"They got into a cab, Winston payin'—he's a perfect gentleman—an' drove to Downin'-street. Mr. Askwith was waitin' there to meet 'em.

"'I hope you're not nervous,' sez the right hon, gentleman.

"'If I was nervous,' sez me father, 'I shouldn't have stood—'

"'They all say that,' sez Mr. Askwith, very gloomy.

"Me father was shown into the ante-room.

"'Here's somebody you know,' sez Winston, 'allow me to introduce you—Brother Clarence—Brother Lloyd; Brother Lloyd—Brother Clarence.'

"'Welcome Brother Clark,' sez Lloyd, 'glad to see you—I hope you're not nervous?'

"'No,' sez me father, 'I've left me money at home an' I'm wearin' a Waterbury watch.'

"Brother Lloyd looked at me father very steady, but said nothin'. By-an'-bye other brothers came in. Brother Haldane lookin' very well in his boy scout uniform, an' Brother M'Kenna in a navy blue suit with pearl buttons.

"'Welcome Brother Clark,' sez Brother M'Kenna very heartily, 'I hope you're not nervous?'

"'If I'm nervous,' sez me father hastily, 'it's because I'm thinkin' of them Dreadnoughts yez forgot to build.'

"Soon after there was a gen'ral move to the lodge room. The followin' account of the formal proceedin's are taken from the Downin' Street Echo an' Cabinet Times:

"'The High Prime (Brother Askwith) took the chair, an' declared the Cabinet opened. "'The minutes of the previous meetin' was read an' confirmed, The financial secretary (Brother Lloyd) brought up the case of Brother Birrell, who refused to pay his subscriptions. Moved by Brother Winston, seconded by Brother Clark, that a letter be written to Brother Birrell. (The High Prime pointed out that as Brother Clark had not been initiated, he was not entitled to second the resolution.)

"'Brother Winston called attention to the fact that the Ex-brother H. Gladstone would soon be leavin' them—(hear, hear). He thought they ought to show him some mark of appreciation—(hear, hear.) He proposed that a cigarette case, suitably inscribed, "from a few friends," be presented, and that there be a farewell smokin' concert, Brother Clark seconded. (The High Prime again pointed out that Brother Clark could second nothin'.)

"'Brother Lloyd George moved an amendment that the presentation be an ash tray with a Chinaman's head—(hear, hear)—an' a suitable inscription: "When this you see, remember me."'

"The amendment was carried nem con.

"'Brother Burns read a letter from Mr. K. Hardie askin' to be proposed for membership. Brother Burns said he couldn't recommend the gentleman. Numerous other letters were read from other gentlemen desirin' membership. Brother M'Kenna moved an' Brother Clark seconded that their letters be burnt. (The High Prime drew Brother Clark's attention to the fact that as he hadn't been initiated a proper brother, he couldn't second no resolutions.)

"'Brother Clark was duly initiated.'

"'I hope you're not nervous,' sez Brother Burns, as me father was led outside into the ante-room.

"'If you say that again,' sez me father very savage, 'I'll pull your whiskers.'

"They left me father alone in the ante-room for a bit; then by-an'-bye Bro. Haldane an' Bro. Bunn come out.

"'Right noble friend,' sez Bro. Burns very impressive, 'do you wish to be a member of the Rare an' Remarkable Cabinet of Downy Birds, fully fledged, an' of the Right Sort—if so answer "I do".'

"'I do,' sez me father; 'what d' ye think I'm waitin' here for?'

"'Right noble friend,' sez Bro. Burns, more solemn than ever, 'do you promise that you will never reveal the secrets of the Cabinet or go gassin' about the country tellin' people what we do?'

"'It ain't likely,' sez me father.

"'Answer "I do",' sez Bro. Burns sternly.

"'I do,' sez me father.

"'An' with that they blindfolded me father an' led him through the door.

"There was a horrible janglin' crash as he set foot in the room.

"'What's that?' sez me father, startled. "'That's Consols a-fallin,' sez a holler voice. "He'd no sooner spoke than there was a shockin' shriek.

"'What's that?''sez me father, more startled than ever.

"'That's a tame suffragette wot we keep on the premises,' whispers Bro. Burns. 'She won't hurt you—she'll feed out of your hand.'

"They led me father up in front of the Grand Prime.

"'Miserable man,' sez the High Prime, 'what seekest thou?'

"'A fat, easy job,' sez me father.

"'Seekest thou admission to the Rare and Remarkable Cabinet of Downy Secretary Birds, fully fledged, an' of the Right Sort?'

"'I do,' sez me father.

"'Say after me,' sez the High Prime, an' uttered a horrid oath:

"'May my food cost me more; may I spend me days buildin' Dreadnoughts, an' me nights eatin' black bread an' horseflesh sausages; may I tax the foreigner, an' vote for conscription if I ever round on a pal, or give a vote to a Suffragette.'

"Then the bandage was took off me father's eyes an' all the brothers crowded round to shake hands.

"'You're one of us now,' sez Brother Lloyd very hearty. 'You're a brother the same as me.'

"Me father drew him on one side.

"'Who's the cashier?' he sez confidential.

"'I am,' sez Bro. Lloyd, an' me father whispered somethin'.

"'Certainly!' sez Bro. Lloyd. 'If you step round the corner with me to the tea-taxin' department, or the sugar taxin' depot, I'll draw a bit for you on account—after all, you deserve it for the fight you've made against them cursed food taxers.'"

VII

A CABINET CRISIS

"I have told you," said Nobby Clark, "how me father won the election for the patriots. I have told you how by means of Clark's Poll Producer me father swep' the country; how he turned out ballot papers already marked with a X, an' how in consequence of his highly patriotic behaviour he was brought into the Cabinet.

"The day after that, when me father was swaggerin' along the Strand—well, not exac'ly swaggerin', but, at any rate, staggerin'—who should he run up against but Austen.'

"'Hullo, Clarence,' sez Austen, shakin' him very affably by the hand, 'How's the game?'

"'Fine,' sez me father.

"'Let's go down the Coal Hole,' sez Austen, 'an' have the Tail of the Dog that Bit Us.'

"So down into the Coal Hole they went.

"'It's a curious thing,' sez Austen, musin'ly, 'that our exports of whisky have risen from £26,000,010 7s. 4d, in 1873 to—'

"'Don't talk shop,' sez me father.

"Austen smiled sadly.

"'Talkin' about shops,' he sez, careless, 'What about your Poll Producin' Factory?'

"'What about it?' sez me father.

"'Well,' sez Austen, more careless than ever, 'I thought we might do a deal; I want a little factory of that sort. We're extendin' our figure department.'

"Me father thought a bit, an' after a few minutes' cogitation—I think that was the name of the drink—me father did a dead, an' went back to the Cabinet to finish up the evenin' pleasantly. It was after the Cabinet was havin' its final drink that night that Winston tipped me father the wink.

"'Wait for me an' Lloyd, after all the others have gone.' he sez, an' me father was wise to the tip.

"By-an'-by, just as M'Kenna was sayin', 'Come on Alec, just a very last final one, an' 'Brother Ure was remarkin' sadly, 'Ah could na tak' anither theembleful but if ye inseest—,' in come the Usher of the Black Rod, an' sez, very stern, 'Time, gentlemen please! Act of Parliament, gents.'

"'Wait for me,' whispered Winston.

"There was a little delay outside owin' to one of the Under-Secretaries wantin' to sing the Land Song, but they got him away quietly in a cab.

"'Come on,' sez Winston, an' him an' Lloyd an' me father slipped round the corner.

"'We're goin' round to the uniform store to see if we can find you a rig out,' sez Winston. 'If we leave it till to-morrer, some of the other fellers will nip in an' pinch the best jobs.'

"'Lots of people,' sez Winston, as they turned into a buildin', 'I don't know why this place is called the Treasury; it got the name owin' to its bein' the place where all the Ministers clothes are kept.

"He opened the door with a key, an' Lloyd struck a match.

"'Step, sof'ly,' whispered Winston, 'or else we'll wake the Great Seal—he sleeps on the premises, but I daresay he'll be chained up at this hour of the night—s-sh!'

"They crep' up the stairs very gashli,* an' Winton unlocked a door. By the light of Lloyd's wax match me father saw the name on the door: CROWN SUITS.

[* Nobby evidently means the Zulu equivalent for "quiet—softly."]

"'This is the crib,' sez Winston, an' turned on the light.

"It was, as me father sez, a very plain-lookin' room, hung with pictures of sportin' events, an' other actresses, but there wan no sign of uniforms. "'Half a mo',' sez Winston, an' pressin' a button a big panel opened in the wall. Inside was a sort of cellar filled with clothes of all descriptions, thrown about in all directions. Gold an' silver uniforms, gold-laced trousis, swords, an' glitterin' decorations, lay in heaps. "Me father picked up one of the diamond stars absent-mindedly, an' put it in his pocket.

"'Put that down, Clarence,' sez Winston, smilin' sadly, 'it's only made of Paris Diamon's.'

"He got inside an' began chuckin' out the uniforms.

"'Here's a War Secretary's trousis,' he sez—'any good?'

"'Too big,' sez me father.

"'Here's Grey's boots—I'll try 'em on meself,' sez Winston; but they was too big also.

"It was a hard job gettin' a suit to fit me father, because every time Winston got hold of a good-lookin' outfit he tried it on hisself first, an' what with him an' Lloyd admirin' themselves in the glass, an' strikin' attitudes gen'rally, me father didn't get a show.

"'How do you like me in this Prime Minister hat?' sez Winston.

"'You look sweet,' sez Lloyd; 'but have you had a dekko at me in this here coronet?'

"'I like them War Office trousis,' sez Winston, thoughtfully; 'they're a bit big, but they're bein' worn big just now, an' I could run a couple of pleats up the side on me sewin' machine.'

"'Do look at me,' sez Lloyd, puttin' an a collar, 'Who do I remind you of?'

"'I forget his name,' sez me father, 'but he used to perform at the Hippodrome, wear dress clothes, an' drink beer like a human bein'.'

"'How do you like me in this naval uniform?' sez Winston. I'd make a good First, or Second-on-the-Right Lord of the Admiralty—pass me that telescope, Clarence; I want to see how I'd look in a picture.'

"'Whilst you fellers are lookin' yourself over,' sez me father, 'I beg respec'fully to call your attention to the fact that I'm gettin' cold feet.'

"So after a bit they got out a kit for me father. He tried it on, so it fitted like a glove.

"'What's this?' sez me father.

"'That's the uniform of the President of the Bored an' Paid,' sez Winston; 'its rather pretty but you'd better wait an' see if John Burns wants it.'

"After rummagin' an hour the only kit they could find for me father was the cast-off suit of me noble frien', Norman, who was unavoidably detained in Wolverhampton.

"'We'll have to make a new place in the Cabinet tor you,' sez Lloyd. 'What do you say to bein' the Official Persuader?'

"'What's the duties?' sez me father. "'You've got to persuade the Irish to keep quiet if we forget to introduce Home Rule. "'It seems an easy job,' sez me father, 'What's the pay?'

"'Four poun' a week an' a free insurance coupon,' sez Lloyd, an' me father took the job.

"'All we've got to do now,' sez Winston, 'is to sit down an' wait for Clarence's Poll Producer to finish the good work.'

"'What?' sez me father, turnin' pale; ain't the elections over?'

"'They're as good as over,' sez Winston, very confident; 'there's only about three hundred more seats to be declared—.'

"'Hot row!' sez me father, fallin' into a diamond-mounted arm-chair—they were still in the Treasury. 'Horrow,' he sez.

"'Why, what's the matter, Clarence?' sez Lloyd an' Winston together.

"'Nothin' at all,' sez me father, in a very holler voice; 'I've been eatin' tipsy cake, an' it don't agree with me.'

"'They all tip-toed out of the Treasury together, with their clothes under their arms. They heard the Great Seal moanin' in his sleep, but didn't disturb him, an' me father, sayin' good night to the other chaps, went off to the House, an' fell into what I might call a troubled sleep.

"Next mornin' he rose an' washed himself—he was so worried that he didn't know what he was doin'— then made his way to the Cabinet Room.

"All the others was there, an' when me father saw how puzzled they looked, his heart went down into his boots.

"The results was comin' in.

"'Hello,' sez the high Prime, who was readin' the paper, 'The cursed food taxers have won another ten seats—magnificent! We're doin' well. Clarence, are you good at arithmetic?' "'I am,' sez me father.

"'Well, sit down an' write a leadin' article for our dauntless Press;' an' after a few instructions, me father wrote one of the finest leadin' articles that ever crep' into a paper.

"'The result of the pollin' (sez a high-placed member of the Government) fills us with joy. We are goin' from victory to victory. We lost ten seats yesterday, which shows that the country is still behind us— with a boot. On Tuesday we lost twenty-one—a significant an' hearty blow at the Bread Burglars. A glance at the follerin' figures will convince the intelligent reader even more than it convinces the intelligent writer:—

Patriots elected 125
Grub graspers elected 134
Net Strength of Patriots 239

Gains an' Losses.
Patriotic gains 2
Food filchers gains 94
Net Patriot gain 96

Analysis of Parties.
Patriots 8.7
Horsemeaters 6.4

"'(It will thus be seen that the Patriots have more than 2 stone the best of the weights.) "'What does this prove? (asks our correspondent). It all depends. It proves we're in the right: it proves we are winnin'. It proves that the country is solid. It proves that those who don't vote for us are potty headed: it proves everythin'.'

Our Majority Is Better Than It Was In 1796!

"We've got more Patriots in Parliament than we had in the days of Oliver Cromwell. England has woke up!'

"But it's a anxious time, all the same. The Cabinet meets an' unmeets. Every few minutes Winston dashes out an' buys a ha'penny paper. Sometimes its full of bright cheerin' news from Haydock Park, sometimes there's nothin' except these rotten elections in it.

"'I can't understand it,' sez the High Prime; 'I can't understand these here glorious victories we're havin'. Here's another two seats gone over to the Black-Breaders—we're doin' fine.

"'I can't understand it meself,' sez me father. "'Anyhow,' sez the High Prime, 'we'll win the Dental Division of Toothboro,' he sez, rubbin' his hands, 'I've just sent down some horse-meat sausages. They'll be the talk of the town,' he sez; 'they was talkin' before they left London.' "'Quite right,' sez me father.

"'An' then,' sez the High Prime, enthusiastic, 'I've got Alec, me Right Hon. friend, to say a few words about pensions—the seat's safe.'

"'I hope so,' sez me father, miserable.

"Just then, in came Lloyd with a paper.

"'High Prime,' he sez, very tragic, 'we've lost the Dental Division of Toothboro.'

"'Heaven,' sez the High Prime. "'Here's the figures,' sez Lloyd:

Food Faker 1,972,846
Patriot 1,211
Majority 1,971,635
Food Faker Gain.

"The High Prime looked an' looked,

"'They seem to have scraped in,' he sez (thoughtful), 'by a narrer majority. Anyway, he sez, 'it only proves we've got the country behind us.'

"'Yes,' sez Lloyd, 'we'll get Clarence to do an article on it.'

"So me father sat down, an' wrote:

"'Once more (writes our Man on the Spot) we have to record a gallant victory for the opponents of Scotland, Wales, an' Ireland. The result of the Dental Election is now to hand. The Patriot polled 1,211.

In 1906 he only polled 1,209.

In 1900 he polled 1,208.

This steady progress in the direction of honest an' fearless legislation must be a bitter pill for the Lords to swaller. What does it mean? We pause for a reply. It means that our majority will be bigger than it was in 1814—the year before the Battle of Waterloo—but not so big as it was in 1885—the year that Peter Jackson beat Slavin.

"Me father's convincin' arguments had their effect. His words were printed in handbill form an' circulated through the country. But it was only for a little while.

"One after another the results began to come in, an' every one was worse than the last.

"An' then the dreadful truth came out.

"Clark's Poll Producer was in the hands of the enemy.

"'Betrayed!' sez the High Prime, claspin' his brow, 'run an' fetch Lloyd, Winston; I want him to swear at Clarence.'

"'Spare me!' sez me father, 'I wanted money!'

"'Dog,' sez Winston, pale an' tremblin'.

"'Traitor!' sez the Right Hon. Redmond, 'an' just as I was buildin' my new palace in Dublin!'

"'Give me two hours,' sez me father, pale but brave.

"'Give him seven years,' hissed Winston.

"Me father left the Cabinet room very hurried. He picked hisself up at the bottom of the stairs an' Winston put his head over the banister and asked if he was hurt.

"'No,' sez me father.

"'I'm sorry,' sez Winston.

"Me father sped east, stoppin' only to buy a penno'th of paraffin oil an' a bundle of wood.

"That night the works of Austen's Majority Developer Company (late Clark's Poll Producer) burst into flames—the Cabinet was saved!"

VIII

"HOME RULE"

"Nobody knows," said Nobby Clark, "what a Cabinet Minister has to go through. When people see a Cabinet Minister ridin' his horse with his gold uniform on, an his sword a-glitterin', an his chain of office round his neck shinin' like a Bovril advertisement, they think that life's a gay dream. Little they know of the sorrerful heart inside that di'mond studded weskit: little they know of the sorrerful feet inside them patent leather boots.

"There was a Cabinet Council called to consider the posish, an' me father went to hit with a heavy heart.

"'Long before the hour of our incomparable Cabinet meetin' (wrote the correspondent of the Winston Weekly, with which is incorporated thy Askwith Argus, the Lloyd Lancet, an' the Haldane Herald) crowds began to assemble in the streets of this great Metropolis. They came from East an' West, North an South. They came from North-East, North-West, South-East by East an' a point South—in fact, they came from everywhere. Thousands, millions, trillions, assembled on the sidewalk. There was at least twenty people in front of Mr. T. Smith's outfittin' store. (By the way, our respected feller townsman has got a new supply of pink socks in—they should not be missed.)'

"Old Sol was shinin' brightly in the sky, gildin' the domes an' roofs of this great city on which the sun never sits, when the first strains of a band announced the comin' of the Cabinet procession. The order of the 'Pageant of Imperial Thought' as one bricklayer in the crowd wittily described it, was as follows:— (Take in programme.)

Detachment of Police.
(under our respected Inspector Sogg).
Band of the Boys' Home.
Fire Engine.
Band of the Irish Band of Hopin' Against Hope. Detachment of the 1st Royal Chinese Crackers.
Mare Bearer.
Carriage containin' (inter alia)
HIGH PRIME: RT. HON. ASKWITH
(Lookin' apprehensive behind him).
Escort of Irish Constabulary.
Mr. John Redmond with an Axe.
Mr. William O'Brien with another Axe.
Two Police separatin' same.
Fire Escape.
Hose Bearers.
Keeper of the Asbestos Suit.
Carriage containin':
RT. HON. URE (whistlin' the George Washin'ton Post).
Escort of Servile Agricultural Labourers (English).
Escort of Thrillin' Scottish Heroes.
Escort of Thrillin' Welsh Heroes.
Band of the 1st Epsom Welchers.
Ten Dukes in chains, cryin' bitterly an' eatin' leeks.
Pand of the Carnarfon Poroughs Look You (Welsh).
Pand of the Eistetfod Whatteffer (Welsh).
RT. HON. LLOYD
(thinkin' deeply with a sade smile).
Escort of Jimmy Welsh.
Band of 1st Limehous Confusiliers.
Ten Trumpeters.
Ten Gold Footmen from Blenheim Palace.
Gold Stick in Waitin'. Gold Stick not in Waitin'.
Other Sticks.
Keeper of the Reversible Coat.
Recorder of Speeches.

Tame Photographer.
Ten Private Trumpeters.
Carriage Drawn by Twelve Performin' Elephants,
containin':
RT. HON. WINSTON
(Lookin' Pale with the Care of Office). Escort of the Pretorian Guard. and of the Hoxton Soup Kitchen.
Band of Clark's Labour Colony. Chief Stone Breaker from Holloway.
Chief Oakum Picker from Wormwood Scrubbs.
Keeper of the Casual Ward.
Band of the Amalgamated Workhouse Masters.
Band an' Banner of the Ticket-of-Leave.
Men's Protection League.
Carriage Drawn by Excited Populace containin':
RT. HON. CLARENCE CLARK
(Very busy dodgin' bricks).
Escort of Warders an' Turnkeys.
Motor-'Bus containin' the rest of the Cabinet.

"'Gentlemen,' sez the High Prime when the Cabinet was safe inside the Lodge room, an' the door was tiled—' Brothers,' he sez, 'we are met to decide—'

"There was loud knockin' at the door.

"'Who's that?' sez the High Prime, gettin' pale.

"'Brother Redmond,' sez me father, who was on duty at the door.

"'He ain't a brother—yet,' sez the High Prime, gettin' paler an' paler.

"'He sez he must come in,' sez me father.

"'Turn the hose on him,' sez the High Prime, an' unloose the dog.'

"'He sez he's got a valentine for you,' sez me father.

"'Tell him to take the fuse ont an' leave it at the War Office,' sez the High Prime.

"There was a long silence which was broke only by the round of beatin' hearts. Bimeby the High Prime sez:

"'Has he gone?'

"'Yes,' sez me father, an' the High Prime looked very relieved.

"'I don't want you to think,' he sez, pullin' himself together, 'that I'm scared of him, only—only just now I ain't anxious to talk about me private affairs. Now, brothers,' he sez, 'we've met today—'

"Bang! went a knock at the door.

"'Arrah!' sez a voice, 'Och be jabbers!' "'Say I'm not here,' see the High Prime, whisperin'.

"'Come out an' be kilt, ye divil,' sez the voice. 'If ye don't lave the dhure open, I'll be afther kicks' it in, d' ye mind?'

"'If that ain't the Ulster Dooley,' sez Mr. Askwith, in a holler voice, 'it's me right hon. friend, Tim Healy.'

"It wasn't a nice Cabinet meetin', because every time the High Prime started talkin', somebody knocked at the door. Sometimes it was the Irish Party, sometimes it was an innercent an' enthusiastic young' feller who wanted to know when the duty was comin' off tea; sometimes it was a deputation of unemployed askin' whether they could have the black bread an' horsemeat sausages that was left over from the campaign; sometimes it was an anti-slavery expert that wanted to know when the Gover'ment was goin' to cancel the New Hebrides agreement.

"The High Prime got so wild that he sent me father out to talk to 'em.

"There was quite a crowd waitin' outside.

"'What d'ye mean,' sez me father, very indignant, 'comin' here an' disturbin' the Cabinet?'

"'If you please, right hon. sir,' sez an ole feller with spectacles, 'we want to know when the Lords are goin' to be smashed an' will there be any tickets issued for the public to see the horrid process?'

"'Go away,' sez me father, very stern; 'you ought to be ashamed of yourself, a man of your age. The Lords ain't goin' to be smashed.'

"'But you said they was,' sez the ole feller, very wild.

"'I know we did,' sez me father, 'but we was speakin' in paraboles.'

"'What's that?' sez the ole chap.

"'A parabole,' sez me father, 'is an election picture—only it's in words.'

"'But aren't you goin' to take away their veto,' sez the ole man.

"'We are,' sez me father, 'when we can find it; at the present moment they've hid it under the bed.'

"'Look here,' sez a young chap with glasses, 'I'm the organisin' secretary of the People Land Brigade.'

"'Loud cheers,' sez me father.

"'What I want to know is,' sez the young feller, 'when is the Lords' land goin' to be handed over to me an' me mates in Hoxton?'

"'We haven't got the exact date fixed,' sez me father, 'but it'll either be Thursday or Friday.' "'When?' sez the feller.

"'March the 21st or 22nd,' sez me father. "'What year?' sez the feller.

"'Anny Domino, 2876,' sez me father—'or thereabout.'

"'But I thought you was goin' to confiscate it at once,' sez the young feller, glarin' at me father.

"'So we was,' sez me parent, 'but they won't let us.'

"'I'd like to ask this right hon. chap,' sez a fat man, 'if the Gover'ment is goin' to keep its promise in re pubs?'

"'Certainly,' sez me father, who had no more idea of what the promise was than the man in the moon.

"'What about the Welsh Church?' sez another feller.

"'We'll do that, too,' sez me father. "'Do what?' sez the feller.

"'I don't know,' sez me father—'anythin' you like.'

"Whilst he was talkin' he heard a suspicious movement behind him. He turned, but too late: he had left the Cabinet door ajar, an' he caught a glimpse of a feller slidin' through the door.

"Me father dashed in after him, closin' the door behind him, but alas! the deed was done! Right Hon. Redmond was inside.

"What a scene of horrow met me father's eyes! There was the High Prime, pale but determined to sell his political life very dear: there was Winston stickin' a bit o' shamrock in his hat: there was Lloyd an' brother Ure standin' like the little princes in the Tower with their arms round one another's necks.

"'What about Home Rule?' sez the Right Hon. Redmond, feelin' the edge of his axe.

"'What's that?' sez the High Prime innercently—'a new kind of temp'rance bev'rage?'

"'Home Rule?' sez Brother Lloyd in a wonderin way; 'what a curious name! Is it a racehorse?'

"'Home Rule,' sez Brother Ure, knittin' his brows, 'I seem to have beard them words before. Is it the name of them servile an' spiritless agricultural villagers that I've been talkin' about?' "'You promised me Home Rule,' sez Right Hon. Redmond, 'an' if I don't get it—'

"'Look here,' sez Brother Askwith gainin' courage, 'let's talk this matter out sensible: don't let there be any unpleasantness. If I happened to mention Home Rule,' he sez, very frank, 'in a moment of excitement—'

"'When you wasn't quite yourself,' sez Winston, suggestive.

"'When I wasn't quite meself,' sez the High Prime.

"'Owin' to a bad attack of influenza,' sez Lloyd.

"'Of course, owin' to me head bein' a bit whizzy; if,' sez the High Prime 'I said any words—an' mind you I don't say that I did—that'd give you the impression that I was talkin' about Home Rule—'

"'You was,' sez Mr. Redmond, very wild; 'you know you was, be jabbers!'

"'Are you sure I didn't say somethin' about horse-meat sausages?' sez the High Prime, very anxious; 'I admit it sounds like Home Rule.'

"'You sez,' sez Mr. Redmond, very dogged 'that if we got you into Parliament, an' helped you to chuck out the Budget you'd give us Home Rule.'

"'Me pore friend,' sez the High Prime, very sad, 'you re not quite right in your head. What I said was—'

"'Look here,' sez Mr. Redmond, very fierce, 'are you goin' to give us Home Rule or ain't you?'

"'At present,' sez the High Prime, cautious, 'we're so busy arrangin' the Cabinet that we haven't had time to give it a thought; if you'd call round in about ten years' time we might discuss it. Home Rule!' sez the High Prime, very indignant, 'I'm surprised at you askin' for it, Mr. Redmond, at a time like this. S'pose I give it you; s'pose I let all you chaps go back to Ireland with a bucket of sulphur an' a box of matches to start a little Parliament of your own? Where the devil has my majority gone to!' "'Home Rule, indeed!' sez Mr. Askwith, gettin' madder an' madder, 'I want Home Rule for England—my Home Rule: an' I can only have it so long as you Irish chaps are safe at Westminster.'

"'What are you goin' to give us then?' sez pore Mr. Redmond.

"'Have a cigar,' sez the High Prime."

IX

SETTLING THE LORDS

"There's ways," explained Nobby Clark, thoughtfully, "whereby it's possible for a party—I'm talkin' of political parties—can prove it's got a bigger majority than the other fellers. Me father invented it.

"When the disgustin' food taxers used to get out their tables of results they did it somehow this way:

Very Liberals 201
Societies 36
Naturalists 80
Other Parties 3
Total—320

Solid Food Taxers 280

"It was left to me father to upset their solidness. One of the first things he did was to classify 'em:

Ordinary Food Taxers 123
Bald-headed Food Taxers 27
Irish Food Taxers 12
Food Taxers with False Teeth 100
Food Taxers (Various) 18

"The elections bein' practically all over, most of the Cabinet is off to them cursed Protection countries, where people live on donkey meat. Lloyd is in Paris studyin' the risin' tide, Winston's in Swizzleland viewin' the giddy heights, the High Prime is stayin' at the Reveriera thinkin' things over. Brother Ure has run across to Lyons' an' is livin' en pension—to use a foreign expression—an' only me father remains to look after the Government, an' to see that the door's locked an' the cat's put out every night.

"It's a tryin' position.

"Before the High Prime left, he took me father aside.

"'If anybody calls whilst I'm away,' he sez, confidential, 'an' sez that I've promised 'em any-thin', just tell 'em that it's receivin' me earnest thought. If the man calls from the poster department, give him a few ideas; if you see Mr. Redmond comin' in this direction open the cellar flap an' ask him to drop in. But whatever you do, try to think of a way for settlin' the business of the Lords.'

"It wasn't long after the other Cabinet chaps had gone before me father's troubles began.

"He'd made hisself comfortable in Downin' Street; he'd laid in a barrel o' beer, a dozen clay pipes, an' a gramophone, an' was preparin' to pass the time pleasantly, when the street door bell went 'ting.

"In came the footman.

"Beg pardon, right hon. Clarence Clark,' he sez, 'but Mr. Hoog, the respected member for the Daisy Division of Michelmas wants to see you.'

"'Show him in,' sez me father.

"In comes Mr. Hoog, a very stout chap with a watch chain you could anchor a ship with.

"'How do, right hon. sir?' he sez, very affable; 'just happened to be passin', so thought I would call in.'

"'Quite right; sez me father; 'have a drink?' "'No thanks,' sez Mr. Hoog, very pleasant.

"Him an' me father sit facin' one another, an' neither of 'em says anythin' for a long time, then Mr. Hoog clears his throat.

"'Very distressin' situation,' he sez.

"'Very,' sez me father.

"'Hardly know what we shall do with these Lords,' sez Mr. Hoog.

"'I don't either,' sez me father, an' there was another long silence.

"Bimeby Mr. Hoog clears his throat again. "'I've got a plan for settlin' 'em at once,' he sez, quite enthusiastic.

"'Have you?' sez me father, cautious.

"'Yes,' sez Mr. Hoog. 'I got the idea in the middle of the night, jumped out of bed, an' wrote it down.'

"'Fine,' sez me father.

"'Yes,' sez Mr. Hoog, modestly. 'I thought you'd be a bit took back.'

"There was another yard of silence.

"'Yes,' sez Mr. Hoog, thoughtful, after a bit, 'this plan of mine is a good one; it'll settle the Lords proper. What you've got to do,' he sez, confidential, 'is to make a lot of chaps Lords.'

"An' with that he steps back to see the effec' of his words. Me father kept wonderful calm.

"'Take a number of trusted members,' sez Mr. Hoog, 'fellers 'who've served the party faithful for years an' years—I've served it faithful meself for ten years—take fellers with a bit of money put by—I've got a bit put by meself—an' make em Lords. See the idea?'

"'I see,' sez me father.

"'If Mr. Asquith should ask you,' sez Mr. Hoog, carefully, 'you might tell him I've got a bit of property at Walthamstow, an' as I'd like to take me title from me property—'

"'It's as good as done,' sez me father. 'You're Lord Hoog of Walthamstow. There'll be a fee of a guinea for enquiries.'

"'Mr. Hoog paid an' went away highly delighted, an' me father prepared to settle down for the evenin'. He was soakin' his clay pipe in beer when 'ting' went the street door bell, an' the footman came in.

"'Beggin' your pardon, right hon. Clarence Clark,' he sez 'but the honourable member for the End Division of Fagshire desires an audience with thee.'

"'Admit him, varlet,' sez me father, an' the member for Fagshire came bustlin' in.

"'Ah, Hon. Clarence,' he sez, shakin' me father warmly by the hand, 'I was just passin', an' it struck me that I might as well call in to tell you of a plan I've thought of for settlin' the Lords.'

"'Yes,' sez me father.

"'Yes,' sez the member for Fagshire, 'it come on me, in a manner of speakin', unexpected. I was walkin' along the Strand wonderin' whether it wouldn't be cheaper to take a 'bus, when all of a sudden—pop!—the idea came!'

"'Dear me,' sez me father, sympathetic.

"'The idea is this,' sez the member for Fag-shire, very impressive; 'let the High Prime make a number of new Lords. Hundreds of 'em—thousands of 'em! There's plenty of patriotic chaps like meself who'd be willin' to be lorded. Take me, for instance. I live in a little place called Brixton. How would it sound: Lord Brixton of Lavender Hill?'

"'Splendid,' sez me father.

"'Of course,' sez the member for the End Division of Fagshire, in a modest manner, it's not meself I'm thinkin' about; it's only our glorious party. At a time like this we oughtn't to think about ourselves, ought we, right hon. sir?'

"'No,' sez me father, 'you oughtn't.

"'Well, what do you think of me plan?' sez the member.

"''Wonderful,' sez me father; 'it's the most sacrificin' thing I've ever heard tell of,' he sez. "'Here are you willin' to be one of them horrible Lords, willin' to allow people to say rude things about you, an' put your picture on a poster—' "'I don't mind,' sez the hon. member, bravely. "'I know you don't,' sez me father. 'All right,' he sez, 'I'll put your name down. Me fee's ten guineas, payable in advance. It'll be returned to you when you get your title.'

"'The old feller went away highly pleased, but not so pleased as me father.

"Me father had hardly settled hisself down before in came the golden footman.

"'Askin' your pardon an' grantin' your grace, right hon. Clarence,' he sez, 'here's the hon. member for Mudshire called in a hurry.'

"'Show him in,' sez me father, wearily.

"In comes the member for Mudshire. "'Sorry to trouble you,' sez the gent, 'but I fell over a good idea this mornin'—'

"'Lord Mudford of Mudshire, sez me father prompt, 'an' the fee is twenty pounds.'

"By the time the Cabinet got back me father was a rich man.

"He hadn't time to tell the High Prime all that'd happened, because Parliament was opened an' everybody was busy. Me father was here, there, an everywhere, an' the way he carried on the duties of Whip—owin' to the regrettable absence of the feller who'd got the job—was the admiration of the Cabinet.

"Perhaps two or three fallers 'd be standin' about in the lobbies talkin'. P'raps some of 'em would be skylarkin'. Suddenly a horrid silence fell on the gay assembly, an' a whisper would run round.

"'Here comes the Whip!'

"You'd see a rush to get out of his way, but he usually managed to get one or two smart ones in. Me father got quite famous in the House owin' to this habit of his, an' when one day the rumour went through the lobbies that he'd been run over by a motor-bus there wasn't a dry eye in the buildin', an' people who hadn't laughed, for twenty years had to be carried to the refreshment room.

"Parliament was in full swing; me father's duties was multi-what-d'ye-call-it; party feelin' run high. Day an' night the House was crowded; me father couldn't get a wink of sleep. Would the Lords be smashed? Would their veto be destroyed? Would the Irish members support the Budget?

"In the Cabinet there's a bunch of trouble. A special lodge meetin' of the Imperial Cabinet Co-op. Society is called for Tuesday night to consider the yearly balance-sheet an' directors' report. Sez the Cabinet Times:

'Bro. Askwith took the chair at 8 sharp, an' on the meetin' bein' called to order an' the minutes of the previous meetin' confirmed, the treasurer brought up his annual report.

'Bro. Lloyd said the tradin' account for the year showed a very satisfactory increase over previous years. Although their Chinese department was now practically at a stan'still owin' to public fashion havin' changed, the directors had opened a donkey-sausage store, which was an immediate success. Thanks to the enterprise of Bro. Ure they was able to report that the Legal Advice (free) Department was in a flourishin' state owin' to the number of pensioners who required information (Cheers.) The directors had laid in a large stock of Dukes (slightly soiled), which they hoped would be a source of profit to the society.

'A Shareholder: I understand there's not much of a demand for dukes.

'Bro. Lloyd: You must leave that to us. (Applause.) The treasurer went on to say that the society would have to write off a lot of depreciation. Norman was gone, Pease was gone, Seely was gone, but they still had him (the treasurer).

'The society then resolved itself into a Cabinet lodge, an' proceeded to the election of officers.'

"'Before we go any further,' sez me father, 'I'd like to say that I consider meself a fit an' proper person to be Governor of the Bank of England an' Master of the Mint. I therefore propose Bro. Clarence Clark tor them offices.'

"'I'm afraid there's no seconder to that,' sez the High Prime, 'an' the motion it lost.'

"'Then,' sez me father, 'I beg to propose Clarence Clark, Esq., as High Prime, an' to move a vote of thanks to the retirin' High Prime for his past services—that's fair.'

"'Pardon me, look you,' sez Bro. Lloyd, 'there's other people who want that job.' "'That's so,' sez Bro. Winston.

"'Then,' sez me father, 'I beg to bring to the notice of the honourable Cabinet a new scheme for settlin' the Lords. (Sensation.) I thought it out meself,' sez me father, modest, 'whilst I was havin' a cup of tea at Lyonses.'

"'What is it?' sez everybody, excited. "'Make a new lot of Lords,' sez me father; 'there's lots of good fellows who'd take the job. Make hundreds of 'em, thousands of 'em.' "'Splendid idea!' sez the High Prime. "'Clarence, you're a marvel—who do you suggest for a start?'

"'Well,' sez me father, a bit bashful, 'it's not for me to say—self praise I never could abide, but how does Lord Clark of Clerkenwell strike you?'"

X

CLARENCE CLARK'S BUDGET

"Could me father be made a lord?" said Nobby Clark, resuming the remarkable story of the rise of Clarence Clark, M.P.—"would the High Prime give him his stripes an' promote him to the Lords' Mess?

"This was the question that agitated the country.

"The papers was full of it. The Lords' Weekly News published me father's photograph with a line under it:

"ASKWITH'S REVENGE."

"The Anarchists' Family Journal an' Sunday Reader was filled with references to me father. There was a column called 'Answers to Enquirers' that was 'specially interestin':

"ANXIOUS ONE: Yes; it's the same Clarence Clark, only he's shaved his moustache off. No, he has always been a traitor to the cause.

MOTHER OF SIX: We cannot advise you to call your latest Clarence. Charles Peace is a prettier name.

WORKER: You would be perfectly justified; fill the bomb with French nails, 3ozs.; Broken glass, 6ozs.; Tin tacks (enough to make into a creamy paste).

Rub the ingredients well together an' drop the whole on to the right hon. gent's head as he is leavin' the "Cabinet Arms."

YOUNG FENIAN SPORTSMAN: No, there is no close time for Clarks: We cannot recommend chloroform; it is too painless.

"But them that feared me father goin' to the Lords hadn't any cause to worry. He knew hisself better.

"'What's the good of me makin' you a lord?' sez the High Prime, 'when I'm goin' to abolish 'em?'

"'But suppose you don't abolish 'em?' sez me father.

"'Then there isn't any need to make you a lord,' sez the High Prime, 'an it took me father hours an' hours to work the answer out.

"But the truth was, me father was too valuable to be wasted in the Lords.

"Every minute of the day he was bein' consulted by the fellers in the Cabinet.

"Sometimes it'd be Winston wantin' him to discuss the weather: sometimes the High Prime would send for him to lick a few stamps—he was here, there, an' everywhere.

"Me father was the handy man of the Cabinet. He mended the chair that Mr. Haldane sat twice on, he whitewashed the backyard, he put the Lie-nolium down in Mr. Ure's office, he cleaned out the Admiralty Press Office, he polished up all the old rifles at the War Office till a Territorial couldn't have told 'em from new ones. In fact, me father made hisself generally useful.

"'You might have a look in at me office, Clarence,' sez Lloyd. 'Clean up them tear stains, an' burn all them speeches I made durin' the war.'

"Nobody knows to this day what happened in the right Hon. Lloyd's office. Some say me father went to sleep at the job an' dropped a candle in the waste-paper basket; some say me father worked so hard puttin' polish into Lloyd's speeches that he set 'em alight. But the general view is that a bundle of speeches went off by spontaneous combustion—for they were a bit hot.

"But the first the Cabinet knew was soon after me father's return to the Lodge Room.

"They was discussin' the Lincolnshire entries in a friendly way when Haldane started sniffin'.

"'What's up, Hal?' sez the High Prime.'

"'Thought I smelt somethin' smoulderin',' sez Haldane.

"'Perhaps,' sez me father, very humorous, 'John Burns?'

"But Haldane kept sniffin' an' by-an'-bye in rushed the Gold Stick-in-Waitin'.

"'Gents,' he sez, with his hair on end, 'Right Hon, Lloyd's office is on fire!'

"'Horrow!' sec Rt. Hon. Lloyd, wringin' his brow, 'The Budget!'

"Everybody ran like mad to the Hon. Lloyd's office, but, as the reporter of the Cabinet Chronicle so touchingly wrote—

"'The conflagration was at its height, an' flames could be seen issuin' from the winders of the doomed edifice.'

"'Save the Budget!' sez Rt. Hon. Lloyd, tearin' his hair—'save me Budget!'

"But, alas! it was not to be—the Budget was burnt!

"Once more was the country in what I might call the throws of a crisis. The Budget was burnt: the only copy of the famous Lord Lamer was lost: Oh, England, my England!

"Hon Lloyd was beside himself, Hon. Winston was Hon. Lloyd, me father was beside everybody. Mr. Askwith looked relieved.

"But what was to be done?

"The Budget was to be introduced the next day.

"'No,' sez the Rt. Hon. Lloyd, answerin' the gifted Lobby Correspondent of the Yippeaddi Llya an' Welsh Advertiser, 'No, I cannot remember what was in it. I know one line started "Whereas," an' another ended "as hereinafter mentioned," but I cannot recall a single line of it.'

"'What will you do?' asked the lobber.

"'We have not decided yet,' replied the thrillin' Chancellor, 'but in all probability we shall induce Rt. Hon. Clarence Clark to make another. He will have to work overtime, but we have every confidence in the right hon. handy man.'

"That was the course the Cabinet decided on. Me father was locked in a room with an exercise book an' a new nib, an' his food was passed through the keyhole. A rubber tube was connected with the barrel an' the other end with me father. Outside the door the Cabinet waited, watchin' the barrel get emptier an' emptier.

"All day an' all night they waited, an' at last as the last drop disappeared they opened the door. There was me father sittin' at the table, a bit dazed but sensible, an' before him was the new Budget—finished!

"That night was one of the great nights of me father's career. The House was crowded; the news had gone round that Clarence Clark would introduce the new Budget.

"What was it?

"Nobody knew.

"Would it tax land? Would it tax beer?

"Them who knew me father best said 'No.'

"Even the High Prime didn't know what it was about.

"'It's goin' to be a popular Budget, sez me father.

"'I've heard of them sort,' sez the High Prime, 'are you taxin' dukes?'

"'Wait an' see,' sez me father.

"Me parent was pale but perfectly sober. As he rose from the Front Bench there was cheers, counter-cheers, an' loud cries of 'No, no!'

"'THE SPEAKER: I now ask Hon. Clarence to oblige with his celebrated Budget.

"'HON. MEMBERS: Yes—no—turn him out—sit down in front—do you mind takin' your hat off?

"'THE SPEAKER: I must ask the noble House to give Rt. Hon. Clarence a chance; keep a little order, can't you? Are you gentlemen of Old England or are you pigs? (Cries of "No, no!") In the name of the Union Jack I call upon Rt. Hon Clarence to oblige.'

"Me father stood like a rock in the path of progress. One hand in his pocket, the other thrust into his weskit whilst with the other he pushed back his flowin' looks.

"'Ladies au' gentlemen,' sez me father, 'feller members an' friends, with your kind permission I will endeavour to introduce to your notice me celebrated Budget, never before seen in public, an' made up by me with me own hands.' (Cheers an' counter cheers.)

"'I have here in me right hand,' continued me father, 'a common or garden Budget: I will turn back the sleeves of me coat an' you will see that I have nothin' concealed; I will hand the Budget round for inspection, an' in the meantime will some gentleman in the audience lend me a hat—?'

"'What are you doin?' hissed the High Prime, 'do you think this is a conjurin' trick?'

"'I had an idea it was somethin' like that,' sez me father.

"'You don't know your business,' sez the High Prime, between his teeth.

"'You don't know me Budget,' sez me father.

"Then he resumed:

"'As I was sayin', me lords an' gentlemen, when me right hon. friend stuck his nose into the conversation, I have here in me head a little Budget—'

"Me father cleared a place on the table.

"'If the Usher of the Black Rod will kindly lend me his walkin' stick, I will endeavour to pass the Budget from this table to the House of Lords without detection. I will then bring the Budget back again without any alteration. (Applause.) Whilst me young friend Winston is takin' a collection, I will endeavour to amuse you by tyin' meself up in knots. Gentlemen,' sez me father, as Winston started off with the hat, 'the pleasin' an' novel entertainment I bring before you to-night is well worth sein'. After I have concluded me own performance, the High Prime will do his famous sword-swallerin' Trick, an' me right hon. friend Ure will give his celebrated recitation—

"I come from Table Mountain,
An' my name is Truthful James."

"I don't know how the entertainment would have gone off," reflected Nobby, "but me father never got a chance of puttin' his novel idea into what I might call execution. There was loud cries of 'Speech!' an' Read the Budget!'

"'Very well,' sez me father, warnin'ly, 'if you insist, you shall have it.'

"The history of Clark's Budget is well known. It was one of the celebratedest Budgets that ever budged. Books have been written about it—mostly comic books. Speeches have been made, an' also songs sung.

"It begun this way:

"Me lords an' common people,—Me relations with foreign Powers are very friendly. The weather has been very fine, but there's been an outbreak of German measles in book form.

"'We have recently acquired four Dreadnoughts an' a new carpet for the drawin' room—(cheers)—but new the kitchen fire still smokes.

"'The country has recently been passin' through a crisis, but the crisis has suffered more than the country.

"'We have made arrangements for Ally's Comet to be on view in a couple of months, but Rt. Hon. Ure's tale won't be on view till the next General Election.

"'Me lords and gentlemen.

"'Dinner is served.'

"There was loud an' enthusiastic cheerin' when me father picked up the Budget an' began to read it. It was a new Budget, labelled all over, 'Fragile,' 'Stow away from boilers,' 'Do not use dog hooks,' an' 'This side up.'

"'We are face to face,' sez me father, 'with the fact that we've got no money. There's lots of ways of gettin' it. We might steal it—(cheers)—we might borrow it from them cursed dukes—(cheers); we might pawn the piano, but we won't. (Cheers.) We want £4,000,000 1s. 11d. for the Army an' £6,000,000 3s. 7d. for the Navy, an' the only thing we're got towards it is a few election addresses an' eightpence.

"'Gentlemen,' sez me father, 'Scotland an' Wales an' Ireland want keepin' an' they have sent their fearless representatives to Parliament to demand that the servile an' spiritless Saxons should raise the money for their old age pensions. (Cheers.) If they had any money themselves they wouldn't trouble you, but this year's haggis crop has been a failure, an' all the leek trees have been nipped by the early frost, an' the shamrock harvest has been a bad one.

"'I ask you, gentlemen,' sez me father in ringin' tones, 'to give generous support to these noble fellers who have voted solid for their counties. If you pass me Budget, they've kindly agreed to lettin' you buy your own Dreadnoughts. Me friends in Ireland will allow you to import your motor-car free of duty. Me friends in Wales will agree to you workin' for your livin', an' me friends in the Whisky Constituency of Macnabshire will continue to tax your tea. Could anythin' be fairer? (No, no.)

"'I have got,' sez me father, 'to raise ninety millions of money for these patriotic countries. (Cheers.) How shall I do it?'

"There was what I would call a great silence. People held their breath: them that hadn't any breath held the other feller's.

"'I propose,' sez me father, 'puttin' a tax of £100 on election addresses—(sensation); a super-tax of £10 each on every promise made in election addresses; a tax of £5 on every political speech; an' a super-tax of a sovereign on every offensive remark made in them speeches. (Uproar.) In this way,' continued me father, I hope to raise £20,000,000 more or less.

"'I propose to put a tax of 6s. 8d. on every lie told durin' elections, an' a duty of £100 on every lawyer standin' for Parliament—this brings me grand total up to £60,000,000. I shall put another tax of £50 on all parsons who make political speeches, a tax of £100 on all newspapers that call Liberals "Socialists," an' a similar tax on all papers that call Conservatives "Food Taxers"—this will bring in another £30,000,000.

"'In this way,' sez me father, 'I shall raise the money without addin' to the cost of livin'. I also propose—'

"'He got no further, for the High Prime rose, pale an' tremblin'.

"'Mr. Speaker,' he sez in a shakin' voice, 'I beg to move that the Right Hon. Clarence be locked up! Me duty,' sez the High Prime, speakin' with great emotion, 'is to abolish the House of Lords: me right honourable friend Clarence is proposin' a Budget that would abolish the House of Commons. (Cheers.) He ain't taxin' the country; he's taxin' us!'"

XI

"QUESTIONS AND ANSWERS"

"Me father," said Nobby Clark, "wasn't the sort of feller that got his head turned by bein' in office; he didn't forget his friends. If you happened to meet my father comin' out of the Downin' Arms or the Asquith Head, he didn't pretend he'd never seen you before, he didn't say, very haughty. 'Excuse me, I know your face but not to speak to.' That wasn't the kind of man he was. He'd shake you warmly by the hand an' take you back into 'The Jolly Winston' or the 'Ure an' Crown,' or whatever pub was handiest, an' let you stand him a drink in as friendly a way as you could wish.

"That was why me father was so popular. The first thing he did when he was made Right Hon. was to send for me Uncle Joe an' appoint him Earwig Catcher to the Treasury; me Cousin Peter, bein' a distant relation, he made First Penwiper to the Second Secretary of the Third Lord of the Admiralty; me Uncle Augustus he appointed Assistant Sorter of the Imperial Waste Paper Basket.

"So, in a manner of speakin', when the crash came, an' me father was in disgrace with the High Prime over his little errow concernin' the Budget, he had what I might call the permanent officials behind him.

"'No, Clarence,' sez the High Prime, sadly, 'you ain't much of a flyer as a Budget Booster; useful as you are to me an' me Cabinet, Lloyd'll have to take his old job an' we'll have to find a new one for you. How would you like to be Chief Answerer?'

"'What's that?' sez me father.

"'Well,' sez the High Prime, 'whenever Parliament meets, there's always a lot of old fellers who've got to get their names in the paper somehow. You see a lot of 'em have spent two or three weeks explainin' to their constituents that if they return 'em to power they'll start reformin' the Empire.

"'Naturally,' sez the High Prime, 'these pore deluded people buy the papers to see what their members are doin' in the Empire Reform business, an', no transactions bein' recorded, they begin to lose faith. You see, Clarence, we haven't got time to allow all the 670 reformers to get to work. We can't even allow 'em to speak on the subject, so they have to ask questions.'

"'What sort of questions?' sez me father.

"'Oh, any sort,' sez the High Prime, careless, 'so long as their names are spelt correct; questions about policemen, an' floods, an' railway accidents. There's a feller who only asks questions about Egyptian crocodiles—he's the Secretary of the Ancient Insects' Protection League; there's another that specialises on lifeboats. They've all got some special point, an' never get away from it.'

"Them words sunk into me father's heart. He took on the job of High Answerer, an' the next day a mysterious advertisement appeared in all the papers:—

"TO MEMBERS OF PARLIAMENT.

WHY ASK SILLY QUESTIONS?

If you want to get your names in the papers, write to Clark's Question Bureau, what'll supply you with new an' interestin' questions never before asked in any Parliament!!

To be up-to-date, you must throw away the old

Bagdad Railway Question;
Irish Constabulary Question;
Forcible Feedin' Question;

AN' TRY

CLARK'S CORKERS.

A sample question warranted to make a Cabinet Minister's
hair stand on end will be sent IN A PLAIN ENVELOPE for

ONE SHILLIN'.

See that the name "Clark" (one "k") is on every sample.

"The success of Clark's Bureau was, in a manner of speakin', instantaneous. Letters arrived by every post, an' me father kept a staff of clerks busy cashin' the postal orders.

"One of the questions me father sent to every client was:—

To ask the High Prime if the time hadn't arrived to introduce the metrical system into England.

"Another was:—

To ask the High Prime to lay on the table a return showin' the increase of beer consumption durin' the general election.

"Another was:—

To ask the First Lord of the Mutual Admirability whether the strength of the Navy would not be increased by enlistin' more sailors.

"But the most important of all was:—

To ask the High Prime to consider the question of increasin' the salary of the Right Hon. Clarence Clark.

"That question was asked 460 times in one week, an' as me father was Lord High Answerer he always replied very encouragin'ly.

"Me father was at his best at question time.

"I don't know," said Nobby cautiously, "whether you understand how the House of Commons is run. You don't? Well, I'll tell you. After all the fellers are in the House, an' the doors locked, the Speaker gets up an' sez:

"'If anybody's got any question to ask the Right Hon. Clarence Clark, let him speak now or for ever hold his peace.'

"After that, the proceedin's may be gathered from what I would term a perusal of the Cabinet Crisis an' Newsletter:—

Mr. W. H. Slobb (Mid-Channel Division of Seaford): I would like to ask the Right Hon. Clarence a question that's just occurred to me. Has his attention been called to the condition of the Gobi-road outside Pekin, an' does he know that it is unsafe for motorists? Will he lay on the table the correspondence between the Liverpool Watch Committee an' the Chief Constable? Will he inform the House how many Dreadnoughts, placed end to end, would reach from Whitehall Berlin? (Cheers an' counter cheers.)

Right Hon. Clarence Clark: In answer to the first question, the Government can either answer Yes or No. (Cheers.) In regard to the second an' third, I must refer me hon. friend to me speech on swine fever of July, 1863. (Cheers an' counter-cheers.)

Mr. Slipper (Inkboro', N.W.): Can the right hon. gentleman inform me: (1) How to use up old candle ends? (2) How to take grease spots out of a fur-lined petticoat? (3) Who was the author of them touchin' lines—

Little Willie had a mirrer,
An' he licked the silver off.

(Hear, hear.)

Right Hon. Clarence: My reply to you is (1) Boil two ostrich's eggs till they are hard, whip a pound of butter into a thick paste, add a pint of hot rum, an' serve hot, garnished with almonds. (2), The flounces should be worn very full, with two guests on each revere; the skirt should be cut in open work panels, an' trimmed with sequins. (3) I would advise you to see a doctor, but in the meantime take the followin' mixture when you've nothin' better to do—

LIQ. ARSENICALIS...1oz.
TINCT. OPII...1oz.
ACID SULPH...1oz.
AQUA PURA...None

A SCENE.

Mr. Chickweed (Mangol Division of Wurzel): I would like to ask the Right Hon. Clarence if he is aware that when I came into the House I had a watch—?

Right Hon. Clarence (warmly): I am. (Cheers.)

Mr. Chickweed: I was goin' to say— (Cries of "Withdraw.")

Right Hon. Clarence: It is a monstrous suggestion. (Uproar.)

The Speaker: Order, order, I shall name the day. (Cheers an' counter-cheers, durin' which the hon. member for Wurzel made remarks which did not reach the gallery.) Right Hon. Clarence (speakin' with great emosh): Durin' all me Parliamentary career I have never heard an hon. member suggest such a thing before, (Cheers.) I hope the incident is now closed. (Cheers.) I admit I was speakin' to the hon. gentleman in the Lobby—(Cries of "Oh, oh!")—but I'm willin' to be searched. (Cheers.)

Mr. Balflour (risin' amidst scenes of unparalleled disorder): I think that is a fair offer. I move for a Select Committee to search Right Hon. Clarence Clark. I may add that I have lost me gold-rimmed glasses an' a diamond niblick presented to me by me admirers. (Uproar.)

The Speaker: Order, order; I shall give it a name in a minute. (Sensation).

Right Hon. Winston: I do hope this matter will go no further. (Cheers,) If me friends would only look after their things, they wouldn't lose 'em. (Right Hon. Clarence: "Hear, hear!") I move a vote of confidence in Right Hon. Clarence.

A division bein' demanded, the followin' was the result:—

For the vote of confidence...201
Against...200
Government majority...1

(Cheers.)

Right Ron, Clarence was deeply touched by this almost unanimous vote, an' expressed hisself in a few well-chosen but eloquent words.

Mr. Chickweed (risin', amidst profound silence): May I say that I am so impressed with Right Hon. Clarence's speech that I shall be glad if he will keep the watch—(sympathetic cheers)—an' accept this gold albert to wear with it? (Loud an' prolonged applause.)

"Me father's reputation rose by leaps an' bounds after this incident, an' the High Prime called a special lodge meetin' to decide what should be done to me father. There was many suggestions put forward in me father's absence—but then me father, like every other great man, had a lot of enemies.

"Whatever would have been decided nobody knows, for just about that time there arose the 94th Cabinet crisis, an me father, as Official Persuader to the Irish party, was called in hurriedly.

"The particulars of that crisis are set forth, as the sayin' goes, at length an' even longer, in the Cabinet Critic (Page 47). Sez that journal:

Another situation has developed. Once more is the Cabinet threatened by Mr. Asquith's ragged an' irresponsible followin'. Once more do the Molly, Macguires an' the Sons of Rest harass the flea-bitten flank of the Cats'-Meat Government.

"On the other hand, the Cabinet Times an' Courier sez:

Another situation line developed. Once more our fearless Cabinet is considerin' with statesmanlike patience a slight hitch in the harmonium of government. Yesterday Mr. T. P. O'Connor, wearin' the same top hat an' frock coat he wore when tourin' America, an' wearin' glover on the very hands he used in collectin' the stuff from our Transatlantic cousins, called on the Right Hon. Clarence Clark an' was immediately ushered into the presence of the great statesman. He came out after a hour with his hair slightly ruffled an' his face scratched, but otherwise optimistic.

"No," he sez, answerin' a question put by our dauntless reporter, "it was a business visit. I am thinkin' of startin' a new paper entitled 'Mainly About Clarence,' an' I was discussin' the details." At half-past six, Mr. T. P. O'Connor, accompanied by Mr. John Redmond, returned to Right. Hon. Clarence's house, an' ten minutes later the police was called in. What does this foreshadow? At nine o'clock a police ambulance dashed up to the front door of Right. Ron. Clarence an' the street was cleared of people.

Afterward, there was a consultation between Mr. T. P. O'Connor an' Mr. John Redmond at the Charin' Cross Hospital, their beds bein' put side by side for the purpose.

At 10-15 Right Hon. Clarence Clark, walkin' with a slight limp, called on the Premier, an' was allowed to sit in the Hall. At eleven o'clock he returned to his official residence. At 11-15 Mr. Tim Healy an' William O'Brien called on the Right Hon. Clarence an' left a bunch of flowers. Right Hon. Clarence addressed them from an upper window. All this is significant of the strength of the Government in 'these tryin' times.

The situation is complicated this mornin' by a speech delivered by Mr. What's-his-name, the leader of the Labour Party for the day.

He said, inter alia:

"I hear...well, if that is so...all I have to say is..."

At 10 o'clock a.m. the nineteen leaders of the Labour Party called on Right Hon. Clarence, but were met by a strong force of police an' turned back. The situation is strained: so is Right Hon. Clarence's leg.

"What is the crisis about? What is the cause of the trouble? Why does the Right Hon. Asquith wear a pale an' troubled dial? Why does me father draw his salary in advance an' prepare to hide himself in the cellar? All this will be disclosed in me next instalment."

XII

THE DEBATE

"The story of me father's crisis," said Nobby Clark, continuing the history of his distinguished relative, "has never been truthfully told, an' ain't likely to be.

"From certain records found in me father's possession when the police searched our house in Downin' Street, an' certain other records said to be discovered by Dr. Wallace, of Nebraska, the celebrated Shakespeare finder, it appears that the crisis started at a Cabinet meetin' held on a Tuesday night. It reads like a story.

"The High Prime was sittin' in a big armchair in front of the fire smokin' his pipe an' wearin' hie slippers. Rt Hon. Winston an' Rt. Hon. Lloyd was playin' a jewette on the pianner, me father an' M'Kenna was playin' dominoes.

"It was a pretty picture—one that'd bring tears to your eyes. All was peace an' harmony, the High Prime beatin' time to the planner with his long clay pipe an' Haldane playin' with a box of soldiers in the corner of the room.

"'What a night!' sez the High Prime. 'How the wind howls round the ole gabbles, an' the rain dashes against yon casement. Clarence, throw another log on the fire an' brew another bowl of cocoa.'

"'Ay, ay, me lord,' sez me father.

"'On such a night as this,' sez the High Prime musingly, 'the good ship Rosebery went ashore in Cordite Bay. I remember it as though it were yester e'en. You were a child then. Right Hon. Winston an' Right Hon. Lloyd was not aboard the old lugger. I was in the fore top-gallant mast bailin out the ship with a bucket when the cry arose, "Rocks on the starboard bow, sir!" I'd hardly time to scramble up or down, as the case may be, before the leaky old tub piled up on the Brodrick Reef.'

"'They was wild an' woolly times, me lord,' sez Right Hon. Haldane, shiverin'.

"'They was,' sez the High Prime, sadly, 'but they've passed—'

"There came a low knockin' at the outer door.

"'Hullo!' sez the High Prime, takin' his pipe out of his face, 'someone knocks on the outer portal. What poor soul is abroad on a night like this, unless i' faith 'tis that poor soul Norman, seekin' a warm seat.'

"Again came the low knockin'.

"'Unbar the door, Clarence,' sez the High Prime; 'there is a sound of howlin' without—which may be the gale, but is more likely me trusty friend, Swift McNeill.'

"So me father opened the door, an' a drippin' figure staggered in.

"It was Right Hon. Elibank, as pale as a ghost.

"'Treason, me lord!' he gasps.

"'Treason?' sez the High Prime, pale as a candle; 'treason, good lad—nay, nay!'

"'Listen,' sez Right Hon. Elibank. 'To-night, as I passed the ruined mill, I saw Right Hon. Redmond conversin' in whispers with Right Hon. Hardie. They were muffled in their cloaks, but I recognised 'em. As they saw me they slunk away, but in their hurry they dropped a piece of paper.'

"With that, Right Hon. Elibank, a very affable fellow but rather stout, produced a scrap of paper from his doublet, an' handed it to the High Prime.

"Right Hon. Asquith took the paper with a tremblin' hand an carried it to the light. It was a bit of newspaper, an' ran:—

'We shall assume office, an' we shall not hold office unless we can secure the safeguards...'

"The rest was torn.

"The Right Hon. Prime read them cruel words slowly, an when he finished there was hardly a dry eye in the room.

"'So,' sez the High Prime, bitter, 'so they're goin' to rake up bygones, are they? They're goin' to do dirty tricks, are they? They're goin' to put a wrong construction on a few remarks—'

"'Made in the way of a joke,' sez Winston.

"'Made in the way of a joke,' sez the High Prime, indignant, 'an' never intended to be took serious—'

"'Hear, hear,' sez the Cabinet.

"'Words,' sez the High Prime, tremblin' with emotion, 'wot was meant to be comic, an' affable, an' they're goin' to pretend that I was serious!'

"Me father, not knowin' all the inner secrets of the Cabinet, was puzzled.

"'What's it all about?' he sez, an' they told him.

"'Pooh!' sez me father, 'that's nothin'! I wonder,' he sez, thoughtful, 'whether that was what Right Hon. Redmond was tryin' to tell me yesterday when he called on me—is it somethin' to do with a Veto?'

"'It is,' sez the Cabinet, unanimous.

"'Then leave it to me,' see me father, puttin' down the double-six, 'it's you to play, Mac.'

"'But what shall I say to the House, Clarence?' sez the High Prime, wringin' his brow.

"'Leave that to me, Herb.,' sez me father, addressin' the High Prime by his Christian name.

"The next mornin' the storm broke, the Lord Lamers was in revolt. Right Hon. Redmond an' Right Hon. Hardie had done their vile work. The High Prime's innercent words was raked up against him. Sez me learned friend, Jimmie D., in the Enthusiastic Comet:

Are we betrayed? Has the lymphatic an' gerrymanderin' obscurist who gyrates in tortuous terminological coryphantic postures before the holy an' knight-errantic hosts of revolutionary Liberalism deserted? Are the pure-minded, high-spirited an' philosophical Andies of Ulster an' Doolies of Dublin to lose the succulent fruits of their Homeric labours, an' satisfy the overpowerin' thirst of their eager souls with pips?

"Sez the Banchester Hardy 'Un in them weighty words that bring the postage up to tuppence:

Never, perhaps, or seldom, has the wise sayin' of Epictitus: 'Populus voto; no decepti'* been so exemplified as at the present moment.

[* I don't know what Nobby is driving at, but I rather imagine that he has dug up from the back pages of his dictionary, "Populus vult decipi et decipiatur."—"Let the people be deceived, as they wish it!"—ED.]

"Me father now reached what I would call the critical part of his career. In a manner of speakin', the eyes of the world was on him. Parliament waited with one hand on the winder sill waitin' to jump out. There had been a conference of the Labour Party. The thirty-nine leaders met in the bar parlour of the Toilers Arms. Veto or Voto? Which should it be, an why? Budget or Fudge it? The Lords or the Loons?

"There was various other illuminatin' battle cries.

"The High Prime was under a cloud; Lloyd was under the table; me noble friend Redmond was under a misapprehension.

"The situation is serious.

"Would the High Prime drop the Budget an' abolish the Lords?

"Would the Lords stand it?

"It was a thrillin' sight when me father rose in his place an' explained his position. I can't do better than give you a clippin' from The Front Bench Advertiser describin' the whole of that famous evenin':

HOUSE OF COMMONS.

The Speaker took the chair at five o'clock. Right Hon. Clarence Clark, lookin' flushed an' happy, entered the House two minutes later, an' received a rapturous welcome from the eight members present.

Mr. Slodge (N.E. Brixton) presented a petition from the agriculturists of N.E. Manchester askin' for an Act of Parliament prohibitin' slugs livin' on cabbages, an' suggestin' that no slug should be allowed in a cabbage field without holdin' a licence an' wearin' an arm-badge.

QUESTIONS.

Mr. Llewellen Isaacs (Betsy Coed) asked Right Hon. Clarence (1) whether the new commercial treaty between France an' Spain to allow the free access of French polish into Spain an' Spanish onions into France had been concluded; (2) if not, where; (3) or as otherwise stated?

Right Hon. Clarence Clark (Witty Division of Bedlam): In reply to my right hon. friend, whose name I didn't catch, I might say that dogs will be muzzled 'as an' from the 2nd of May. (Ministerial cheers.) I have no information in regard to the condition of unemployment in Iceland. (Opposition laughter.)

AN AMUSIN' SPEECH.

Captain Kettle (North Donnybrook): Whether Manchester Free Trade—(laughter)—or Birmingham Tariff Reform—(loud laughter)—could be introduced into Ireland. (Renewed laughter.)

Right Hon. Clarence Clark: After them witty remarks of the gallant an' learned Cap., I think we will leave it at that. (Hear, hear.)

IMPUDENT QUESTIONS.

Mr. Mudd (Black Division of Pool): Will a Royal Commission be held to inquire into the circumstances of Right Hon. Clarence Clark's election? Is it a fact that he got into the House by tippin' a policeman? (Cheers an' counter-cheers.)

The Speaker: Half-a-moment, young feller; are you aware that you're talkin' about one of the highest respected Right Hons. in the House? (Cheers.) Just steady yourself a bit, or I'll order the Sergeant-at-Arms to give you a clip in the ear with me mace. (Cheers.)

Mr. Mudd: I refuse to sit down. (Uproar.) Right Hon. Clarence: Do you call yourself a gentleman? (Cheers.)

Mr. Mudd: No. (Cheers.)

On the motion of the High Prime, the question was adjourned.

VETO DEBATE.

Right Hon. Redmond, ruin' amidst scenes of excitement, said:

What do you mean by it? What do you take us for? Do you think we're goin' to stand it? I never heard such cheek in me life! Did me right hon. friend say so an' so, at such an' such a place? I believe he did. Do I think he was tryin' to deceive me an' me fellow patriots? I do an' I don't. (Cheers amidst which the right hon. gent. resumed his seat.)

Right Hon. Clarence Clark, risin' to reply, was the subject of an ovation, one of which nearly struck the Right Hon. Friend of Man.

I cannot," sez the noble speaker, "recall any occasion when I'd much rather been home an' in bed. (Cheers.) You have asked me which we are goin' to take first, the Veto or the Budget? (Cheers.) If you'd have asked me to take somethin' else, I'd have answered prompt. (Laughter an' tears.) The reply to the question is this: Have we to pass the Budget or haven't we? (Cries of 'Yes' an' 'No.') Have we to abolish the House of Lords or haven't we? (Cries of 'No!' an' 'Yes.') Well now, look you, if we abolish the House of Lords first, how are we goin' to pass the Budget? (Sensation.) If, on the other hand, we pass the Budget first, how are you goin' to abolish the Veto? Me solution in simple."

There stood the Right Hon. Clarence, calm an' unmoved, 'an the whole House sat silent. On the opposite benches was Balflour an' Austen utterin' loud sneers; below the gangway was Right Hon. Redmond grindin' his teeth. In the Distinguished Strangers' Gallery sat our young friend, Joynson-Hicks, ponderin' deeply. All the members who sat in the House was standin' on the tiptoe of tenterhooks or bein' tossed from side to side by the fog-horn of a dilemma. They hung upon Right Hon. Clarence's words.

"I propose," sez Right Hon. Clarence, slowly, "to get out of the difficulty, Veto first or Budget first, by Vetoin' the Budget."

It was a long time before Right Hon. Clarence could resume. The cheers was deafenin'. From all sides of the House arose deafenin' an' frantic cheerin'. Many of the reporters in the gallery were overcome an' had to be led away to the refreshment room.

Right Hon. Clarence Clark then went on to review the political situation. He dealt with the horrible state of Germany, where owin' to Protection, the Germans was obliged to build battleships an' call 'em cruisers for fear of offendin' England. (Cheers.) How much better things was in England, where they built ships with guns on the trade union system.

"Guns," sez Right Hon. Clarence, proudly, "that refused to work except now an' again. Then take the question of cats'-meat—"

Right Hon. Redmond: Hear, hear.

Right Hon. Clarence: Right Hon. Redmond sez, "Hear, hear!" Does he know that cat's meat is sold by the ton in Germany?

Right Hon. Austen: Who eats it?

Right Hon. Clarence: Cats. (Cheers.) Does me learned friend know that black bread is ate by the hundred ton?

Right Hon. Long: Who by?

Right Hon. Clarence: Undertakers an' people in mournin'. (Cheers an' counter-cheers.) That is the position that the Government has got to face; them are the hard facts that the food-taxers can't stand. In conclusion, I ask you one an' all to rally to the support of your old tried an' trusted Cabinet, who will never desert the party so long as the Civil List pays pensions.

The right hon. gentleman resumed his seat.

DIVISION.

XIII

THE LAST PHASE

"Me father's life in Downin'-street," resumed Nobby Clark, "was one of the happiest times in his life. The Downin'streeters was a quiet, respectable lot of people an' very seldom got into the police courts. There was a time when it wasn't all it mighthave-been, an' when the police used to go down the street in pairs, but most of the bad characters moved away in '06. The Right Hon. Balfourrs-they was terrors—the Right Hon. Austens—they was argumentative fellers—the Right Hon. Longs, an' all that crowd was ejected for not payin' rent, an' a brighter, happier crowd moved in. No more winder-breakin', no more nothin'—just a affable, friendly lot of neighbours.

"Me father lived at 83, the Right Hon. Asquiths lived on the right an' Right Hon. Winstons lived on the left. The Right Hon. M'Kennas had the second floor of me father's house, an' the Right Hon. Haldanes lived opposite.

"The only disagreement me father had was with the Right Hon M'Kennas.

"'Mac,' sez me father one day, 'it's your turn to scrub the passage.'

"'We did it yesterday,' sez Mac, very aggressive.

"'Well,' sez me father, 'it's your turn to wash the steps.'

"'We did that yesterday, too,' sez Mac, very loud. 'If you ask me anythin', Clarence, we do more than our share.'

"'Oh?' sez me father—'Oh?' he sez—'if you're goin' to talk about what you do, I might remind you that we're always openin' the door to your visitors.'

"'That your fault,' sez Mac, 'there's the notice on the door:'

M'KENNA.
Marine Inventor.
KNOCK TWICE.

"'But they knock once twice.' sez me father, very mad, 'instead of knockin' twice once, an' I can tell you that I'm tired of comin' up from me kitchen to lake in insultin' messages from Right Hon. Beresford.'

"But that was the only fly, so to speak, in me father's vaseline, an' them days in Downin'-street was happy.

"There me father would be potterin' about the garden, in an old straw hat, plantin' snowdrops, an' onions, an' other beautiful flowers—or smokin' the earwigs out of the cabbages. On the other side of the wall would be Right Hon. Asquith feedin' the chickens, or paintin' the summer house, singin' away as light-hearted as could be.

"Sometimes me father would climb up on the other wall an' have a chat with Right Hon. Winston.

"Only them who've seen the really great in what I might calll their hours of ease have got any idea how lifelike they are.

"There would be Winston rollin' the garden in his old pink perjarmers, with an old cocked hat on the back of his head, an' a calabash pipe in his month. You'd never think to see him that he was the same dignified young feller that spoke his mind so free about the Lords.

"In the evenin' they all used to meet at the 'Downin' Arms,' a little pub at the corner of the street, an' talk about poultry, an' gramophones, an' similar agricultural pursuits, an' perhaps Lloyd would distribute leek-seeds what he's got sent up from his estate at Llanchillrhwd.

"That's how life went: smooth an' friendly an' in a manner of speakin', brotherly.

"One afternoon when me father had got a few friends in for a big worm hunt, an' the beaters is just startin' off, Right Hon. Asquith popped his head over the wall.

"'Right Hon. Clarence,' he sez, 'what are you doin' to-night?"

"'Nothin' much,' sez me father.

"'Come in,' sez Right Hon. Asquith; 'after the children have been bathed, an' we'll have a bit of a talk about Finance.'

"'Certainly, right hon. sir,' sez me father, presentin' arms with his gun—'I told you there was a worm hunt on, didn't I?'

"That night a small select party gathered in the High Primes front room.

"I'm sorry to bring up this subject again,' sez Right Hon. Asquith, 'but the fact is—'

"Just then the High Prime's servant girl put her head in the door.

"'Anyone here named M'Kenna?' she sez, 'because if there is, he's wanted.'

"'Excuse me,' sez Mac, an' went out.

"He left the door open, an' bimeby me father heard a voice which sounded like Right Hon. Beresford's.

"Look here, Mac,' be sez, 'what about them guns of the Invisible? The front one won't fire, an' the back one won't load; now, what I suggest—'

"We heard the door slam, 'an' in came Mac, lookin' very annoyed.

"Twenty times a day that feller comes worryin' me,' he sez. 'What do I know about ships an' guns? Go on, High Prime.'

"'To resume,' sez the High Prime, 'we've got to settle to-night about the Lords: an' we meet do somethin' about money. The Lords are a national danger,' he sez. 'They're runnin' about wild in the streets, an' bitin' people; they wear coronets, an' they oppress carpenters.'

"'Why carpenters?' sez me father.

"'When I say carpenters,' sez the High Prime, careful, 'I mean the Honest British Workman, who's always a carpenter in the pictures.'

"'The thing to do with the Lords,' sez Winston, 'is to shut 'em up in a duke's palace an' make 'em pay for their own board: charge 'em so much a head. Now,' he sez careless,'I've got a relation who'd do the caterin'—he's a duke, but a very decent feller—'

"At that minute in came the High Prime's slavey.

"There's a feller outside who wants to see M'Kenna,' she sez.

"'How's he dressed?' sez Mac.

"'In a sailor suit,' she sez.

"'It's him,' sez Mac, very desperate; 'what does be want?'

"'He wants a word with you about the Invisible,' she sez. 'One gun won't work, an' one gun won't wash, an'—'

"'Tell him I'm gone to Portsmouth to inspect rivets' sez Mac.

"'But what's more important than the Lords,' sez the High Prime, 'is this here money question—how much have we got left, Lloyd?'

"Right Hon. Lloyd pulled out his notebook.

"'By knockin' of a couple of Dreadnoughts,' he sez, 'we can just manage to pay our own salaries: by disbandin' a couple of regiments we can pay Haldane's extras, an' by other clever economies we can pay John Burns hie extra rise of salary.'

"Everybody was very glum an' silent.

"'It's a pity we couldn't get that Budget through sez the High Prime musin'ly.

"'What?' sez Right Hon. Clarence?

"Now all this time me father was thinkin' furious.

"'Is the game up?' he sez, after a bit.

"'It's only a matter of months,' sez Right Hon. Asquith, an' a low moan broke from everybody as they began to realise the horrow of the position. 'If we only knew a way of raisin' about a million to tide us over,' sez Right Hon. Lloyd.

"'What about Kakadu an' Cackler,' suggested me father; but the Cabinet shook their heads.

"'That'd upset me friends in Wales,' sez Lloyd, 'an' besides, Kakadu's no pinch, an' after Jerry M's disgustin' display at Kempton I'm losin' faith in Cackler.'

"There was another long silence, broke only by the sound o' deep an' earnest thinkin'.

"'I know a way,' sez me father after a bit; 'but,' he sez sadly, 'I don't think the Right Hon. Cabinet has got any confidence in me.'

"'Nay,' sez the High Prime, very reproachful—'nay,' he sez, 'that don't seem fair to your old friends an' supporters.'

"'I know a method,' sez me father, very reflective, 'of makin' that £20,000 go a long way—a method,' he sez proudly, 'of me own invention.'

"'Is it honest?' sez Haldane, cautious.

"'Don't let us deal with side issues,' sez Right Hon. Lloyd—'is it workable?'

"'It's workable,' sez me right hon. father, 'or at least, I hope it is.'

"All the Cabinet wanted to know what it was, but me father refused to divulge his secret.

"'It's me own invention,' he sez, 'an' it isn't properly protected yet. What you've got to do is to get all the money you can together, hand it over to me, shut your eyes an' wish.'

"'That's what I call good sound finance,' sez Right Hon. Lloyd, enthusiastic.

"'An' then,' sez me father, dreamily, 'I shall take the money an' bring me invention into play.'

"'It sounds all right,' sez Winston, 'what happens then?'

"'When I come back,' sez me father, very impressive, 'that twenty thousand will be two million.'

"They nearly fell on his neck.

"'Clarence,' sez the High Prime, in a voice broken or bent by emotion, 'you're the greatest man in the world.'

"'Won't the Tories be wild?' sez Winston, rubbin' his hands.

"'What a lark it'll be to see their faces when we bring the money into the House in sacks an' plank it down on the table,' sez Right Hon. Lloyd.

"'Let's buy a Dreadnought on the quiet,' sez M'Kenna, 'an' call it "the Beresford."'

"They sat there for an hour sayin' what they'd do with the cash.

"'What do you call your invention, Clarence?' sez the High Prime.

"'I call it,' sez me father, 'Clark's Benefit.'

"'That's a fine name,' sez the High Prime, 'I vote we nip round to the Treasury an' collect the stuff now.'

"With that they drunk up an' went round to the Treasury to collect the stuff.

"They was a merry party," said Nobby reflectively, "laughin', jokin', an' pushin' people off the pavement. They got to the Treasury, an' the High Prime opened the door with his skeleton key.

"They went through the office, openin' safes, takin' the money out of the till, an' collectin' all the cash there was to collect.

"'What about the Sinkin' Fund?' sez Winston.

"'It's no good goin' there,' sez Right Hon. Lloyd, very hasty, 'I've been there.'

"Everybody carried as much money as he could stuff into his pockets, an' back came the whole party to Downin'-street.

"They counted it up, an' it came to £19,473 8s. 4½d.

"'Now,' sez me father, 'I shall want a taxi.'

"So a taxi was called, an' me father, assisted by the other Right Hons., put the money in the cab.

"'What you chaps have got to do,' sez me father, 'is to go back into the High Prime's back parlour and wait. When I come back, it'll be with a traction engine drawin' the fruits of me invention.'

"'Shall I come with you?' sez Right Hon. Lloyd, but me father shook his head.

"'That'd spoil the invention,' he sez.

"They all gathered together to give him a send-off.

"'How long will you be?' sez the High Prime.

"'It's doubtful,' sez me father; 'I might be an hour an' I might be longer.'

"Amidst deafenin' cheers the taxi drove off, an' the Cabinet went indoors to wait for me father's return.

"They spent an hour sayin' what a wonderful chap me father was, an' how he ought to be made a Lord, an' how the Lords wasn't worth it.

"'He'll be comin' back, now,' sez Lloyd, lookin' at his watch; 'do you think we ought to get a few fellers in to help carry the money indoors?'

"'Perhaps he wouldn't like it,' sez M'Kenna, an' just then the door burst open an' in dashed Right Hon. Beresford in his sailor's suit.

"'Look here,' he sez, 'I want to ask Right Hon. M'Kenna about them guns of the Invisible.'

"'Right Hon. Charles,' sez M'Kenna, very dignified, 'I can't give you any answer, but as soon as Right Hon. Clarence cornes back—'

"'If you think I'm waitin' till then you're jolly well hidin' up the wrong tree,' sez Right Hon. Beresford. 'As a matter of fact,' he sez, 'I've been talkin' to Clarence.'

"'Where did you see him?' sez the Cabinet all together.

"'At Charin' Cross,' sez Right Hon. Beresford, 'He was gettin' on to the Continental train.'

"Lloyd went pale, an' the High Prime sank into a chair tremblin'.

"'Ain't he comin' back?' he sea in a hollow voice.

"'From what he told me,' sez Right Hon. Beresford, 'you can expect him back in about twenty years' time.'

"In this way," said Nobby Clark, in conclusion, "me father retired from what I might call public life; he was never seen again, though from time to time Right Hon. Lloyd used to receive picture postcard from foreign places tellin' the cabinet that me father was enjoyin' good health. But somehow the state of me father's health never worried the Cabinet."

Edgar Wallace – A Short Biography

Richard Horatio Edgar Wallace was born on the 1st April 1875 at 7 Ashburnham Grove, Greenwich. His mother, Mary Jane "Polly" Richards was born into an Irish Catholic family in Liverpool in 1843 and had worked in theatres, both as an actress in bit-parts and as a stagehand and usherette, until she married a Merchant Navy Captain, Joseph Richards, in 1867. He too had been born into an Irish Catholic family in Liverpool. His father had also been a Captain in the Merchant Navy, and his mother's family had a marine background. Mary was eight months pregnant with Joseph's child when he died at sea, and it was once the child had been born that she first turned to the stage, taking the stage name Polly Richards.

She joined the Marriott family theatre troupe in 1872. It was managed by Mrs. Alice Edgar, Richard Edgar, Grace Edgar, Adeline Edgar and Richard Horatio Edgar, Wallace's father. In late 1874 Mary and Richard Horatio Edgar had a brief sexual encounter at the party following a successful show, and she fell pregnant. Worried about the scandal which would ensue and fearing that she might forever lose her job at the troupe, she fabricated an obligation in Greenwich would detain her there for at least six months. She lived in a room in the boarding house on Ashburnham Grove until her son, Edgar, was born. She had already made preparations through her midwife for a couple to foster the child, and when Edgar was born the midwife presented her with Mrs Freeman. Her husband was a fishmonger at Billingsgate market and she already had ten children. She was happy to foster the child and for Polly to make frequent visits to see him in exchange for a small sum of money which Polly made from her work in the theatre troupe.

Wallace was now known as Richard Horatio Edgar Freeman, taking his father's forenames and his foster family's surname. Broadly speaking his childhood was a happy one. The Freemans looked after him lovingly and he had good friendships with his foster siblings, particularly Clara Freeman, twenty years his senior, who often looked after him as a child. After a few years Polly's finances tightened and she was no longer in a position to afford the fee she had been paying the Freemans. However, they had grown to love the young Wallace and opted to adopt him in order to keep him out of the workhouse. Polly could no longer visit him. George Freeman was keen to ensure that he had equal opportunities and did all he could to secure him an education at St. Alfege with St. Peter's, a Peckham boarding school. Despite his adoptive father's efforts, though, Wallace left the school aged twelve for truancy.

Instead he went to work and by the time he was fourteen or fifteen he had experience selling newspapers at Ludgate Circus, near Fleet Street, as a worker in a rubber factory, as a shoe shop assistant, as a milk delivery boy and as a ship's cook. He stole from the milk company which resulted in his dismissal, and in 1894 was engaged to a local girl from Deptford named Edith Anstree, though he broke this off and instead joined the Infantry. He adopted the name Edgar Wallace which he took from Lew Wallace, the author of *Ben-Hur*, and his medical record records a diminutive 33" chest and a stunted growth. his first posting was with the West Kent Regiment in South Africa in 1896, though he did not enjoy military life, arranging to be transferred to the Royal Army Medical Corps. Though this was a less strenuous job, it was also significantly less pleasant and so he again transferred to the Press Corps, which he found suited him far better.

He was in Cape Town in 1898 where he met Rudyard Kipling and was inspired to begin writing and publishing poetry and songs. His first collection of ballads, *The Mission that Failed!* and was enough of a success that in 1899 he paid his way out of the armed forces in order to turn to writing full time. His first work was as a war correspondent for Reuters who kept him in Africa to cover the Boer War, and then for the Daily Mail in 1900 and various other periodicals after that. It was while he was in South Africa that he met and married Ivy Maude Caldecott, who was 21 when they married in 1901, despite her Wesleyan missionary father's strong opposition to the union, for several reasons, one of which was that Wallace's writing was not turning quite the profit he had expected it would. *War and Other Poems* and *Writ in Barracks,* both published in 1900, had not proved as popular as his first collection. Eleanor Clare Hellier Wallace, their first child, died of meningitis in 1903 and, in rather deep debt, they returned to London. Wallace used his contacts with the Daily Mail to get work with them in London, electing to write detective novels as a means of making quick money.

Wallace met Polly, his birth mother, in 1903. He didn't remember her from his childhood as he had been too young when she became unable to visit, so it was as though they were meeting for the first time. She was sixty years old and terminally ill, living in abject poverty. She had come to Wallace seeking financial support, but he turned her away. She died in the Bradford Infirmary later that year. In 1904 he and Ivy had a son, Bryan. He was still writing and had completed his first thriller, *The Four Just Men*. Since nobody would publish it he resorted to setting up his own publishing company which he called Tallis Press and he published a serialised version of *The Four Just Men* in 1905. He received promotional assistance from the Daily Mail in which he ran a competition for entrants to guess the method of murder in the final chapter, with a prize of £1,000 for a correct guess. Although the paper's proprietor, Lord Alfred Harmsworth, refused Wallace the £1,000 prize money, Wallace persisted and went ahead with the competition, recklessly advertising on billboards and buses all over the country, hoping to expand his advertisements across the Empire. His worried colleagues at the Daily Mail managed to convince him to lower the prize money to £500, split into a first prize of £250, a second prize of £200 and a third of £50, but with the total cost of his advertisements nearing £2,000 he would need to sell £2,500 worth of copies before he could see any profit. He was confident that this could be achieved in just three months.

Though he had remarkable enthusiasm, it became clear that his managerial skills left a lot to be desired. It soon emerged that nowhere in the competition terms and conditions had he included a clause limiting the competition to one single winner; instead, any entrant with a winning answer was entitled to their corresponding prize money. Thus, if ten entrants guessed the first prize answer, the competition was obliged to pay each entrant £250. This error was only noticed after the competition had been closed and the solution had been printed in the final installment of the novel, meaning that not only was there no opportunity to write his way out of enormous financial obligation, but the entrants who had guessed correctly would by now have read the final chapter and know they had done so. £250 was an enormous amount of money to the average Edwardian family and those entitled to it were likely to make a lot of noise if they didn't receive their money. Despite this, Wallace's fist instinct was to attempt to ignore the issue entirely, even as he discovered that he initial calculations had been dramatically over-enthusiastic and it would take nearer to two years of continuous sales to break even at the initial cost of £2,500, let alone the new figure which included every correct guesser. Compounding the problem even further was the awful realisation that as sales continued throughout the initial three month period and Wallace approached the £2,500 break-even figure, new readers were still eligible to enter and guess correctly. Though it is unknown how much he eventually owed his readers, Lord Harmsworth found himself having to loan over £5,000 in order to protect the reputation of the newspaper, since 1906 had come around and there still hadn't been a list printed of all prize-winners. It was less a charitable act than one of a man anxious that the failure would reflect ill on his own paper. Wallace filed for bankruptcy shortly thereafter and as a token gesture to his creditors sold the rights to the novel to Sir George Newnes, a publisher and editor, for £75. In the midst of this chaos though, Wallace managed to write and published *Smithy*, which would become the first of a series of *Smithy* novels.

Following this fiascos Wallace was dismissed from the Daily Mail in 1907 when inaccuracies which were found in his reporting, resulting in libel cases being brought against the paper. That year he became the first reporter to be fired from the Daily Mail and was his awful reputation prevented him from finding work at any other papers. Despite all this, though, he travelled to the Congo Free State later that year and reported on the criminal treatment of the Congolese people by King Leopold II of Belgium and the Belgian rubber companies. Up to fifteen million Congolese were killed in various atrocities, and Wallace was asked to serialise stories based on his experiences for her penny magazine *Weekly Tale-Teller*. He and Ivy had another daughter, named Patricia, in 1908. Though his new work for *Weekly Tale-Teller* was bringing in some money, their financial situation was still dire and Ivy was occasionally forced to sell off her jewellery and possessions in order to pay for food. In 1911 his Congolese stories were published in a collection called *Sanders of the River*, which quickly became a bestseller. He would publish eleven more such collections featuring a total of 102 stories of adventure and tribal life set on the river Congo.

From 1908 he started to enjoy a revival of both his success and his reputation. The majority of his initial writing he sold outright in order to make money as quickly as possible and placate his creditors in the United Kingdom and South Africa, but as his success saw the reestablishment of his reputation he began to find work once again as a journalist, beginning in horse racing for the *Week-End*, the *Evening News* and then as an editor for the *Week-End Racing Supplement*. Following this success he started his own racing papers, *Bibury's* and *R. E. Walton's Weekly*, eventually buying his own racehorses and losing thousands gambling. His success was insufficient to support his newly extravagant lifestyle and his marriage began to fail in the light of his financial irresponsibility. He and Ivy had their last child together, Michael Blair Wallace, in 1916, and she filed for divorce in 1918 moving to Tunbridge Wells with her children.

Wallace began to fall for his secretary Ethel Violet King and they married in 1921, having a child, Penelope Wallace, in 1923, who would herself go on to become a successful crime writer. Wallace now began to take his career as a fiction writer more seriously, signing with Hodder and Stoughton in 1921. He now began to organize his contracts more carefully, arranging for royalties and properly organized promotions, run by people more business-minded than himself. He was marketed as the 'King of Thrillers' and they gave him the trademark image of a trilby, a cigarette holder and a yellow Rolls Royce. He was truly prolific, capable not only of producing a 70,000 word novel in three days but of doing three novels in a row in such a manner. His publishers signed off on almost everything he wrote as soon as he turned it in, estimating that by 1928 one in four books being read at any time was written by Wallace, for alongside his famous thrillers he wrote variously in other genres, including but not limited to science fiction, non-fiction accounts of WWI which amounted to ten volumes and screen plays. Eventually he would reach the remarkable total of 170 novels, 18 stage plays and 957 short stories.

Wallace became chairman of the Press Club which to this day holds an annual Edgar Wallace Award, rewarding 'excellence in writing'. In 1923 he broadcasted a report on the Epsom Derby horse race for the British Broadcasting Company, making him the first ever radio sports correspondent. His ex-wife Ivy had suffered from breast cancer between 1923-1924, and it eventually killed her in 1926 despite a successful operation to remove a tumour the year before. He wrote the essay "The Canker in our Midst" in 1926 which dealt, aggressively and controversially, with the problem of paedophilia in show business, describing how children were unwittingly left open to sexual abuse, and linking paedophilia with homosexuality. Its tone has been described as "intolerant, blustering, kick-the-blighters-down-the-stairs". He was appointed chairman of the British Lion Film Corporation on the back of the success of *The Ringer* and on the agreement that he give British Lion first choice on all his future work. This contract gave him an annual salary and a large amount of stock with the company, along with a stipend on all British Lion production of his work and 10% of their annual profits. This extraordinary contract gave him annual earnings by 1929 of almost £50,000, or almost £2 million in 2014.

He now became an active figure in politics, entering the 1931 general election as a Liberal contestant in Blackpool, rejecting the current government in favour of free trade. He lost the election by over 33,000 votes and went to America in late 1931, once again deeply in debt after buying the *Sunday News* which closed six months later. In America he quickly found work as a script doctor for RKO Pictures, enjoying early success with the 1932 adaptation of *The Hound of the Baskervilles*. This success, along with that of the play *The Green Pack*, established his reputation in America and he was able to see his own work adapted for film, beginning with *The Four Just Men*. His most successful theatrical work, *On The Spot*, which explores the life of Al Capone, has been described as "arguably, in construction, dialogue, action, plot and resolution, still one of the finest and purest of 20th-century melodramas". These successes led to his assignation on RKO's "gorilla picture" which would become famous as King Kong in 1933.

He worked on the first draft though he was beginning to experience severe headaches which brought about a diagnosis of diabetes. Despite taking medication to address his condition, it deteriorated in a matter of days. His wife booked him passage home but soon heard that he had entered a coma and died of his condition and double pneumonia on the 7th of February 1932 in North Maple Drive, Beverly Hills. In his honour the bell at St. Bride's church on Fleet Street tolled for the duration of the morning while the flags flew at half-mast. He was buried near his home in England at Chalklands, Bourne End, in Buckinghamshire. Once again, at the time of his death he was in severe debt, mostly to racing bookkeepers, though these debts were settled within two years thanks to the enormous royalties his estate continued to receive from his contracts. His writing has been translated into 29 languages, and is considered one of the most important bodies of Colonial writing.

Edgar Wallace – A Concise Bibliography

African Novels
Sanders of the River (1911)
The People of the River (1911)
The River of Stars (1913)
Bosambo of the River (1914)

Bones (1915)
The Keepers of the King's Peace (1917)
Lieutenant Bones (1918)
Bones in London (1921)
Sandi the Kingmaker (1922)
Bones of the River (1923)
Sanders (1926)
Again Sanders (1928)

Four Just Men (Series)
The Four Just Men (1905)
The Council of Justice (1908)
The Just Men of Cordova (1917)
The Law of the Four Just Men (US title: Again the Three Just Men) (1921)
The Three Just Men (1926)
Again the Three Just Men (US title: The Law of the Three Just Men) (1929) a.k.a. Again the Three

Mr. J. G. Reeder (Series)
Room 13 (1924)
The Mind of Mr. J. G. Reeder (US title: The Murder Book of Mr. J. G. Reeder) (1925)
Terror Keep (1927)
Red Aces (1929)
The Guv'nor and Other Short Stories (US title: Mr. Reeder Returns) (1932)

Detective Sgt. (Inspector) Elk series
The Nine Bears or The Other Man or The Cheaters (1910)
revised as Silinski - Master Criminal (1930)
The Fellowship of the Frog (1925)
The Joker or The Colossus (1926)
The Twister (1928)
The India-Rubber Men (1929)
White Face (1930)

Educated Evans (Series)
Educated Evans (1924)
More Educated Evans (1926)
Good Evans (1927)

Smithy (Series)
Smithy (1905)
Smithy Abroad (1909)
Smithy and The Hun (1915)
Nobby or Smithy's Friend Nobby (1916)

Crime Novels
Angel Esquire (1908)
The Fourth Plague or Red Hand (1913)
Grey Timothy or Pallard the Punter (1913)

The Man Who Bought London (1915)
The Melody of Death (1915)
A Debt Discharged (1916)
The Tomb of T'Sin (1916)
The Secret House (1917)
The Clue of the Twisted Candle (1918)
Down under Donovan (1918)
The Man Who Knew (1918)
The Strange Lapses of Larry Loman (1918)
The Green Rust (1919)
Kate Plus Ten (1919)
The Daffodil Mystery or The Daffodil Murder (1920)
Jack O' Judgment (1920)
The Angel of Terror or The Destroying Angel (1922)
The Crimson Circle (1922)
Mr. Justice Maxwell or Take-A-Chance Anderson (1922)
The Valley of Ghosts (1922)
Captains of Souls (1923)
The Clue of the New Pin (1923)
The Green Archer (1923)
The Missing Million (1923)
The Dark Eyes of London or The Croakers (1924)
Double Dan or Diana of Kara-Kara (US Title) (1924)
The Face in the Night or The Diamond Men or The Ragged Princess (1924)
The Sinister Man (1924)
The Three Oak Mystery (1924)
The Blue Hand or Beyond Recall (1925)
The Daughters of the Night (1925)
The Gaunt Stranger or Police Work (1925) revised as The Ringer (1926)
A King by Night (1925)
The Strange Countess (1925)
The Avenger or The Hairy Arm (1926)
The Black Abbot (1926)
The Day of Uniting (1926)
The Door with Seven Locks (1926)
The Man from Morocco or Souls In Shadows or The Black (US Title) (1926)
The Million Dollar Story (1926)
The Northing Tramp or The Tramp (1926)
Penelope of the Polyantha (1926)
The Square Emerald or The Woman (1926)
The Terrible People or The Gallows' Hand (1926)
We Shall See! or The Gaol-Breakers (US Title) (1926)
The Yellow Snake or The Black Tenth (1926)
Big Foot (1927)
The Feathered Serpent or Inspector Wade or Inspector Wade and the Feathered Serpent (1927)
Flat 2 (1927)
The Forger or The Counterfeiter (1927)
Terror Keep (1927)

The Hand of Power or The Proud Sons of Ragusa (1927)
The Man Who Was Nobody (1927)
Number Six (1927)
The Squeaker or The Sign of the Leopard or The Squealer (US Title) (1927)
The Traitor's Gate (1927)
The Double (1928)
The Flying Squad (1928)
The Gunner or Gunman's Bluff (US Title) (1928)
Four Square Jane or The Fourth Square (1929)
The Golden Hades or Stamped In Gold or The Sinister Yellow Sign (1929)
The Green Ribbon (1929)
The Calendar (1930)
The Clue of the Silver Key or The Silver Key (1930)
The Lady of Ascot (1930)
The Devil Man or Sinister Street or Silver Steel
or The Life and Death of Charles Peace (1931)
The Man at the Carlton or The Mystery of Mary Grier (1931)
The Coat of Arms or The Arranways Mystery (1931)
On the Spot: Violence and Murder in Chicago (1931)
When the Gangs Came to London or Scotland Yard's Yankee Dick
or The Gangsters Come To London (1932)
The Frightened Lady or The Case of the Frightened Lady or Criminal At Large (1933)
The Green Pack (1933)
The Man Who Changed His Name (1935)
The Mouthpiece (1935)
Smoky Cell (1935)
The Table (1936)
Sanctuary Island (1936)

Other Novels
Captain Tatham of Tatham Island or Eve's Island or The Island of Galloping Gold (1909)
The Duke in the Suburbs (1909)
Private Selby (1912)
1925 - The Story of a Fatal Peace (1915)
Those Folk of Bulboro (1918)
The Book of all Power (1921)
Flying Fifty-five (1922)
The Books of Bart (1923)
Barbara on Her Own (1926)

Poetry Collections
The Mission That Failed (1898)
War and Other Poems (1900)
Writ In Barracks (1900)

Non-Fiction
Unofficial Despatches of the Anglo-Boer War (1901)
Famous Scottish Regiments (1914)

Field Marshal Sir John French (1914)
Heroes All: Gallant Deeds of the War (1914)
The Standard History of the War – Volumes 1 – 4 (1914)
Kitchener's Army and the Territorial Forces:
The Full Story of a Great Achievement (1915)
Vol. 2-4. War of the Nations (1915)
Vol. 5-7. War of the Nations (1916)
Vol. 8-9. War of the Nations (1917)
Famous Men and Battles of the British Empire (1917)
Tam of the Scouts (1918)
The Real Shell-Man: The Story of Chetwynd of Chilwell (1919)
People or Edgar Wallace by Himself (1926)
The Trial of Patrick Herbert Mahon (1928)
My Hollywood Diary (1932)

Screenplays
King Kong (1932, first draft of original screenplay, 110 pages) While the script was not used in its entirety, much of it was retained for the final screenplay.
The Hound of the Baskervilles (1932, British film)
The Squeaker (1930, British film)
Prince Gabby (1929, British film)
Mark of the Frog (1928, American film)
The Valley of Ghosts (192

Short Story Collections
The Admirable Carfew (1914)
The Adventure of Heine (1917)
Tam O' the Scouts (1918)
The Fighting Scouts (1919)
Chick (1923)
The Black Avons (1925)
The Brigand (1927)
The Mixer (1927)
This England (1927)
The Orator (1928)
The Thief in the Night (1928)
Elegant Edward (1928)
The Lone House Mystery and Other Stories (1929)
The Governor of Chi-Foo (1929)
Again the Ringer The Ringer Returns (US Title) (1929)
The Big Four or Crooks of Society (1929)
The Black or Blackmailers I Have Foiled (1929)
The Cat-Burglar (1929)
Circumstantial Evidence (1929)
Fighting Snub Reilly (1929)
For Information Received (1929)
Forty-Eight Short Stories (1929)
Planetoid 127 and The Sweizer Pump (1929)

The Ghost of Down Hill & The Queen of Sheba's Belt (1929)
The Iron Grip (1929)
The Lady of Little Hell (1929)
The Little Green Man (1929)
The Prison-Breakers (1929)
The Reporter (1929)
Killer Kay (1930)
Mrs William Jones and Bill (1930)
Forty Eight Short Stories (George Newnes Limited ca. 1930)
The Stretelli Case and Other Mystery Stories (1930)
The Terror (1930)
The Lady Called Nita (1930)
Sergeant Sir Peter or Sergeant Dunn, C.I.D. (1932)
The Scotland Yard Book of Edgar Wallace (1932)
The Steward (1932)
Nig-Nog and other humorous stories (1934)
The Last Adventure (1934)
The Woman From the East (1934) Co-written By Robert George Curtis
The Edgar Wallace Reader of Mystery and Adventure (1943)
The Undisclosed Client (1963)

Other
King Kong, with Draycott M. Dell, (1933), 28 October 1933 Cinema Weekly

Plays
An African Millionaire (1904)
The Forest of Happy Dreams (1910)
Dolly Cutting Herself (1911)
The Manager's Dream (1914)
M'Lady (1921)
Double Dan (1926)
The Mystery of room 45 (1926)
A Perfect Gentleman (1927)
The Terror (1927)
Traitors Gate (1927)
The Lad (1928)
The Man Who Changed His Name (1928)
The Squeaker (1928)
The Calendar (1929)
Persons Unknown (1929)
The Ringer (1929)
The Mouthpiece (1930)
On the Spot (1930)
Smoky Cell (1930)
The Squeaker (1930)
To Oblige A Lady (1930)
The Case of the Frightened Lady (1931)
The Old Man (1931)

The Green Pack (1932)
The Table (1932)